Starry Night Surprise

By Justin Mitson

Illustrations by Drew Rose

Red Team Ink
DBA of Zealot Solutions, Idaho LLC
5447 Kendall St.
Boise, ID 83706
Copyright © 2016 by Red Team Ink

For permission requests or information about discounts for special bulk purchases please contact: redteamink@gmail.com. Substantial discounts on bulk orders are available to corporations, professional associations, and small businesses.

Printed in The United States of America

Library of Congress Control Number: 2017930049

ISBN: 978-0-9982349-0-8

Title: Starry Night Surprise
Description: First Edition

This book is dedicated to Channing and Charise —
my inspirations for fearless adventure.

Table of Contents

CHAPTER ONE
A FLICKERING FLAME IN THE FOREST

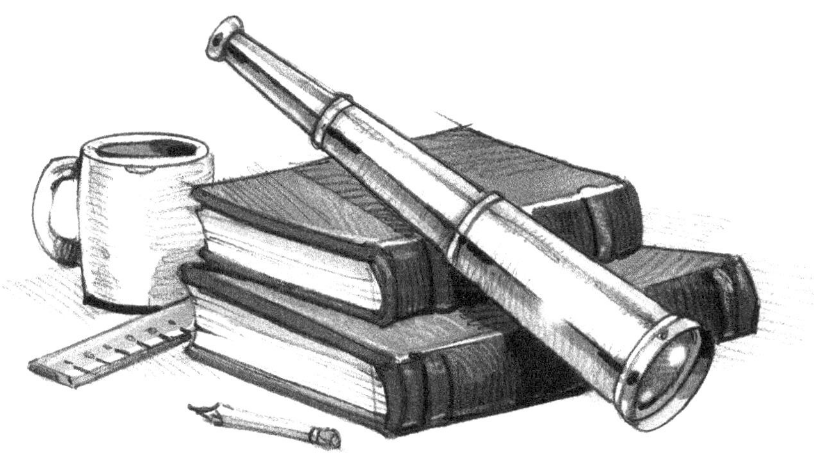

On a beautiful night in the brisk chill of autumn, Snowy enjoyed another session of watching constellations and shooting stars. She loved the way the night sky would come alive with glimmering, beaming lights. She loved it so much, in fact, that she often slept all day, just to stay awake far into the night. Her favorite sight was a meteor shower growing in intensity. It was always glorious!

Her house sat on a hilltop above Epping, a town nestled in a thick grove of trees that made up Epping Forest, where whirling gusts of wind stirred together the scent of fresh pine and forest soil. The uppermost floor of what used to be her grandfather's house had been converted into an observatory and laboratory. Snowy spent most of her time looking through telescopes or microscopes, studying and recording the results of various scientific experiments. In her astronomy notebook, she recorded new stars and other findings for the Royal Observatory. When she wanted to relax, she got comfortable in her favorite overstuffed chair and read science books.

Tonight, just like any other night, as the first stars appeared, her friend Minty stopped by for a visit. Minty appreciated viewing the night skies too, watching in wonder with green eyes that sparkled against pale skin. Mostly, though, she came to talk with Snowy to keep her company. The two girls had known each other since they were two years old, and had spent most of the last ten years becoming the best of friends.

Also like any other evening, tonight Minty made a pot of her piping hot chamomile tea. It helped to keep her friend warm as she worked on astronomy projects into the wee hours. It was a secret recipe that was a tad too sweet, with a hint of warm cinnamon that tickled the nose. Perhaps it was even enchanted, because somehow it always stayed hot and never lost its steam.

Minty poured some into two cups and handed one to Snowy, who wrapped her fingers around the chipped blue mug, inhaling the sweet scent. Her lips curled up into a smile at the thought of having such a wonderful friend. Snowy's home was cozy, yet drafty with age, and tea was the perfect drink with which to warm up on a chilly night like this. Sometimes Minty also brought a few freshly baked cookies, which often left Snowy with a watering mouth, and a desire for even more sweet treats. Minty always seemed to sense when her friend's stomach was growling and ready for a filling snack. She would arrive at just the right time with a basket of delicious fresh-picked fruit or a tray of savory meat and potato pies. Their crimped crusts and small size were perfect for holding in the hand while munching. One such pastry sat in a saucer beside Snowy's chair, and was just waiting to be devoured.

Snowy admired her friend's cooking, thinking she was the best cook and herbalist in all of Epping. The young scientist was always a willing taste tester for Minty's many culinary experiments.

Minty herself lived at the bottom of the hill, just on the outside of Epping. Her English cottage with its thatched roof was covered with overgrown ivy and herbs that reached so high the roof was almost completely hidden. Tall, pink hollyhocks, purple delphiniums, and white daisies created a beautiful border in front of the white-gated fence, and wild red roses cascaded over the arch above the latch that led inside.

Several paths surrounded the cozy cottage. Minty often skipped down one to explore the forest, looking for herbs to

snip for her cooking, singing as she went. Sometimes she would tie ropes around tree branches to glide over bubbling streams, or she would stretch a tightrope over the flowing water, practicing her balance. Whenever Snowy visited, Minty showed off her latest acrobatic feats. So far, she had perfected somersaults and graceful pirouettes on the tiny tether. She'd laugh and do all sorts of daredevil tricks as the light from the sun glimmered across the cool, fresh water.

As the evening wore on, Snowy watched as the moon continued to rise against its canvas of blackening blue, masking the twinkling of some stars in its brilliance. As she watched, she sketched a new telescope design that she'd been working on for several weeks. She yawned while pushing her glasses atop her head, pulling back strands of blond hairs. Minty was already asleep, her head drooping against the rocking chair's cushioned back, and her copper-tinged brunette hair cascading perfectly around her face.

Snowy put her sketchbook aside to peer through her grandfather's telescope. She missed that wise old astronomer, and on this night the loneliness was sharper than usual.

Grandfather had taught her everything he knew about science, and so working in the observatory always made her think of him. She never wanted to forget Grandfather, even though the long days were stacking up since she'd seen him last.

Feeling sleepy, Snowy's thoughts wandered back to that dreadful day when a group of ogres surprised the villagers—the day her grandfather vanished. The ogres had taken the strongest men in the village, Grandfather being one of the first captured. The monsters loved to eat, but they didn't want to work to grow their food, so the men were forced to work in the fields, harvesting for them. The ogres were so lazy they also took many of the mothers from the village to cook their meals.

When Snowy was just a baby, her parents were killed in an accident, and she had lived with her grandfather ever since. Now, Snowy only had Minty, and Minty only had Snowy. Minty's parents, as well as her older brother, had been taken away by the ogres too. The girls did their best to use all their wonderful skills and talents to help the remaining women and children of the village. They encouraged them not to give up, to keep dreaming of the day when they would find and rescue their loved ones.

As Snowy gazed at the sky through the telescope, the peacefulness of the night air was disrupted by the call of unsettled crows. She perked up, knowing crows usually try to sleep at night. She watched with trepidation as a heavy fog crept over the land, and the darkness took on a sinister feeling that was anything but normal. Even though she hadn't the slightest idea what it meant, Snowy could tell that something was *very* wrong.

Snowy's pudgy black and white cat, Galileo, stopped purring in a snap, as his fur bristled and his back arched with tense caution. The natural nightly sounds of Epping Forest suddenly halted, leaving a strange silence about the hilltop and forest below.

Peering again through her grandfather's telescope, Snowy scanned the distant hillside, stopping when she thought she saw a glimmer of light and smoke rising. Pausing to wipe her smudged spectacles, she looked again, and was now certain she saw flames flickering from an open fire. She wondered if there were hunters camping in the forest. She hoped it wasn't poachers illegally hunting on her land again.

Snowy made up her mind that if she found poachers, sleepy or not, she would march straight to the mayor's office and demand that he write a report.

However, after gazing for a few minutes more at the area where the flames flickered, her eyelids became heavy and she suddenly felt very tired. Snowy curled up on her window seat, wrapped her arms in a snug embrace around Galileo, and went to sleep, worries forgotten.

Chapter Two
Warning the Townspeople

As the sun rose the following morning, bathing the hills in tones of muted yellows and pinks, Snowy started the morning bread. She yawned, polishing the spectacles she'd fallen asleep in *again* last night, and winced when she realized that she'd mistakenly put salt in the bowl instead of sugar. She did just great when mixing chemicals in her lab, but often made mistakes when baking, and even when dressing herself. Just this morning, she'd sleepily put her favorite blue trousers on backwards, and her white tunic on inside out! It was probably because her mind was always preoccupied with her next experiment.

At least Minty didn't see the mistakes, since she had apparently gone home earlier that morning. Snowy wished she had even half of Minty's talent for baking. Nevertheless, she comforted herself with the reminder that each person has his or her own special gifts, and baking was just not one of hers.

After she corrected her mistake and set the bread aside to rise, Snowy turned the telescope in the direction of the smoke and flames seen just a few hours before. Flames which, oddly, had seemed to lull her to sleep. Now that the sun was peering over the mountaintop, she could see large shapes moving around a dim fire that puffed out wisps of smoke. The realization of what she saw filled Snowy with a chill that froze her to the very spot where she was standing, her blue eyes round with terror.

Giant shapes, like enormous human beings, stood, stretching and yawning. They were the largest, nastiest-looking group of creatures she had ever seen, and even though they were quite a distance from Snowy, they were rather intimidating. She didn't need to be close to them to imagine their sharp fangs and massive, threatening muscles.

Snowy mentally gathered her courage and focused on what she saw through the telescope lens, trying her best not to think about how horrid the creatures looked. It seemed they were packing up camp. They gathered weapons and belongings, and slung packs over their broad backs as though they were about to embark on a hike. They doused the fire with water from oversized tin cups. As she watched them pack, it occurred to Snowy that these beings must be the very creatures she'd dreaded to think about her whole life—ogres!

Much to her dismay, it looked like they were lumbering down the winding trail toward Epping.

Doing some quick math in her head, Snowy calculated that the ogres could reach Epping in less than an hour. There was no time to waste!

She bolted for the front door with bare feet, jetting over the cobblestone path, squishing through the dew-kissed grass and down the dirt path to Minty's house. All she could think about was that with each passing minute, the ogres were getting closer to Epping and the beloved townspeople that were like family to her. Then she thought about what the ogres had done to her blood family. She shivered at the thought, but pushed it away at once and focused on the goal she was running toward.

Out of breath, Snowy pounded on the door of Minty's cottage. Her pounding was met with silence. "Minty!" Snowy tried to yell, but only managed to gasp.

After a couple of seconds of heavy breathing on Snowy's part, she heard the rusty latch of Minty's door squeal before the slab of wood swung open. Minty rubbed her round green eyes before running a hand through her tangled mop of brunette waves.

"What in the world are you doing, Snowy?" Minty scowled with a tired sigh. "If this is about another constellation discovery, you're going to have to wait until I've had breakfast and brewed some tea before I can properly pay attention."

"Ogres! It's the ogres!" Snowy tried to shout, but her voice came out small and airy once again. She held out her hand to her friend. "Minty, they're almost here." she gasped. "We have to go now!"

Without hesitation, Minty leaped outside, grabbed her friend's hand, and together they ran barefoot down the road, Minty's light green dress waving as they fled. Galileo scampered along right behind them, and then promptly disappeared, going who knows where. As they ran, they tried to figure out how to warn every man, woman and child that remained from the last invasion. They had to think of the perfect plan, and they had to do it fast.

When they got to the town square, no one was stirring. Snowy and Minty knew they didn't have time to go house to house to warn each family. With a glance at the church, Minty looked at Snowy, and Snowy looked at Minty, exchanging a mischievous wink. They had an idea.

Bolting toward the church, Minty barged, shoulder first, into the wooden door. It flew open and Minty caught sight of the dangling rope that connected to the church bell. She smiled—with a little *too* much excitement—and did something she had always wanted to do. She ran and jumped off a pew, launching herself high into the air taking hold of the bell's rope. The bell resounded with violent gongs as Minty swung back and forth, gripping onto the rope with every ounce of strength she possessed.

The sound of the clanging bell was so loud that both girls wanted to cover their ears, but Minty held on to the rope, toughing it out. Snowy, however, ran outside to escape the ear-splitting chimes.

As Minty kept ringing the bell, Snowy pressed her hands together in excitement. She knew it could be heard throughout the entire town. No one could ignore it, or mistake it for anything other than the church bell, and each and every citizen had to know it meant something serious—especially considering the early hour.

Abruptly, people began to appear, hurrying up the dirty cobblestone roads. Worried mothers with their sleepy-eyed children drifted together in anxious wonder. Snowy looked for Mayor Carol, whom she soon spotted pushing his way through the crowd to get to the church. When he finally made it to Snowy, she told him what she'd seen.

Mayor Carol had avoided being kidnapped with the other able-bodied men during the previous ogre invasion by hiding in his cellar, an act which cost him the respect of many townsfolk. Although he was not the bravest of men, he had been waiting a few years for a chance to redeem himself. He knew this was the perfect opportunity. So the overweight, red-faced man took charge, organizing an evacuation plan.

Within a few minutes of Mayor Carol's plan being explained, many of the townspeople took flight, leaving Epping, headed toward Southend-on-Sea. Snowy was glad that Mayor Carol had finally taken charge, but knew the evacuation was going far too slowly. The ogres would make it to town well before everyone had the chance to flee.

Being her smart self, Snowy had an idea that just might work to stall the monsters...

CHAPTER THREE
SUGARCOATED OGRES

Minty and Snowy asked Mayor Carol to escort the people away to safety, while they stayed behind to slow down the ogres. Having known the girls all of their lives, Mayor Carol suspected they had some crazy idea, but didn't have time enough to stop them. As his new-found courage began disappearing into smoke, he wished Snowy well and ran toward Southend as fast as his chubby legs could carry him.

Not wasting a minute, Snowy and Minty dashed to the bakery near the church and found several dozen huge bags of powdered sugar. They dragged some back to the church, their legs moving in quick, short strides.

As the church bell began to ring erratically, Snowy grabbed an armful of thick twine and several pulleys from a nearby stable. She ran back to the church, and tossed the twine up to Minty, who was busy climbing the bell rope, causing the discordant ringing. Minty climbed all the way to the very top of the church's steeple, right up to where the bell glinted in the early morning sun.

Minty peered out from the steeple's opening. The ogres were getting so close! Some of them were already on Baker Street, just a few blocks from the church. "At least they don't seem to be in a huge hurry," Minty said, watching their big feet slog along.

After Snowy had hoisted the last of eight bags of sugar up to Minty, she darted inside the church and locked the enormous front door. She pushed a pew against the entry, and then another, trying her best not to think about how it might only stop the ogres for a few seconds. Sweat trickled down her temples as she continued on. She just hoped Minty's part of the plan would have more success.

After tying an escape rope to the steeple, Minty positioned all the sugar bags at the edge of the roof. Minty bowed her head, clasped her fingers together, and said, "God, please let this plan work so that the townspeople can be safe."

The ogres approached with slow, steady thumps which rumbled through the town like thunder. Minty motioned to Snowy to climb the rope to the bell. From the square windows of the church's steeple, the girls watched as the dreadfully ugly, twelve-foot tall creatures roared with rage at finding the townspeople gone. The ogres kicked open each cottage door, one by one, in hopes of finding someone, anyone.

They continued to roar their disappointment... until one ogre smiled with wicked pleasure upon spotting Minty and Snowy on the church roof. His yellow teeth were black and rotting at the gums. Snowy thought some dental floss would do him some good. He motioned to an ogre beside him, pointing at the girls.

Minty pulled on the rope of the church bell. The loud clanging got their full attention. At least twenty of them, either holding spiked clubs or oversized, jagged swords, stood in the courtyard, squinting up at Minty and Snowy in confusion. Some of them growled, while others threw their clunky arms up, unsure of what to do next. "Why girls no running?" one grunted.

"Hey, what are you brutes looking at?" Minty called down to them. "Haven't you ever seen two girls on a roof before?"

"What?" The ogres were shocked to hear Minty mocking them. Usually, people ran from them. They weren't accustomed to being made fun of, especially by little girls. Why weren't they afraid?

"Hey, Stink-brain!" Snowy shouted. "I'm the one who warned everyone that you were coming, and helped them all leave! Ha! Now you'll have no breakfast and all the townspeople are safe!" she said before sticking her tongue out at them.

One of the beasts growled, "We get you and eat you for breakfast! You look tasty to me!" When the ogres spoke, their words were slow and forced, as if they really struggled to muster up sentences.

"Oh, no, you won't!" Minty said. "You're not smart enough, fast enough, or strong enough to catch us! I promise you that!" She thumbed her nose at the staring giants.

Snorting and snarling, the leader of the ogres, Krag, stomped to the front door of the church. He had a bruised purple complexion and was just a tad larger than the others, but other than that, he looked equally stupid and just as ugly as the rest. With a single punch of his strong, hairy fist, the lock burst and the door split apart in wooden shards all over the pews.

Snowy called down, "Hey, don't you even know how to properly use a door? Didn't your mother teach you *anything*?"

"Don' no talk 'bout Mama Ogre!" Krag roared, frothing through his under-bite, red-faced and angry. The other ogres guffawed, making Krag even angrier. "You lil' girls in big trouble!" Krag gargled.

When Krag hobbled through the doorway, Snowy gathered up the bell's rope.

"Give me that rope!" Krag hollered while several more of the ogres rushed in behind him. "Give me rope or you be *very* sorry! You no get away with this!" The angry ogre stomped his feet.

One by one, the clumsy creatures jumped, trying to grab the rope. Each landed with a loud thump, their pickle-like fingers empty handed.

The girls couldn't help but giggle at the silly monsters. "Those leaping toads are the most ungraceful ballet dancers I have ever seen!" Snowy exclaimed. They imagined them wearing tutus and ballet slippers, causing a fit of giggling again.

Minty reached into her skirt's hidden pocket and grabbed her lucky penknife. Because it was lucky, she never went anywhere without it, not even to bed. She used the knife to saw at the ropes that held the huge bell in place.

All the while, Krag stared up at them, yelling and shaking his hairy fist. "You be sorry for this! We bigger and stronger than you. We'll eat you alive!"

After feeding the heavy bell-ringing rope through a pulley, Snowy threw it out of the steeple to the ogres in the courtyard. One of them snatched it instantly, and as he did, Snowy stuck her tongue out. Minty cut the last piece of rope that held the bell. As it fell, Minty and Snowy jumped away from the steeple onto the lower roof. So far, their plan was working!

The heavy bell landed with a tremendous thud on Krag's gigantic head, and in doing so, the ogre holding the other end of the rope was launched high into the air, the rope zipping through the pulley. He flew through the sky like a purple comet, eventually slamming headfirst into the side of the church.

As the other ogres scrambled to rescue his stuck and wriggling body, even more ogres appeared from inside the church. Minty and Snowy pushed the heavy bags of sugar over the edge of the roof onto their melon-sized heads below. The bags fell like bricks, knocking out several of the unsuspecting ogres, and bursting into an amazing explosion of white. Huge clouds of powdered sugar swirled in the air, twinkling like pixie dust. The sugar cloud became so thick the panicked ogres couldn't see anything as they gasped and thrashed around the courtyard.

Minty and Snowy repelled down the side of the church on the thick escape rope that Minty had let down earlier. The cloud of white sugar enveloped them as they touched the ground. They darted away as fast as they could, trying not to breathe it in. They ran past the stables and up the street toward their homes. As they ran, Snowy had another grand idea.

"Minty, I've always wanted to try that sugar experiment. It could be really fun!" She paused in her tracks, pointing to a home's fireplace, visible through an open door. "Can you grab that flaming log for me?"

Minty was a bit uncertain, but followed the request. She grabbed the burning log out of the fireplace, careful to hold it by the end that wasn't hot, and took it to Snowy. Not knowing what to say, she handed it to her friend.

Snowy held the log and said, "I read somewhere that fine sugar in the air is flammable, but I've never had a chance to test it." With that, she ran back and threw the log as hard as she could into the chalky, thick haze. Both girls sprinted in the opposite direction. They looked back just in time to see the log crash against the cobblestone road.

Sparks from the burning log ignited the fine particles of sugar in the air. Soon Epping's entire town square became engulfed in a huge fireball. Minty and Snowy were thrown to the ground just outside its reach. Just as fast as the fireball flashed to life, it sputtered out. The girls looked at each other in amazement.

Back at the town square, Krag was no more. Several of the others were seriously injured. Many sported black eyes and bloody noses. All of them were dazed after the air around them exploded into flames.

"Looks like your experiment worked!" Minty said, wide-eyed with wonder.

Snowy agreed, a bit startled as she righted her once-again-dirty glasses on her nose. As they headed back toward the hill from which the monsters had come, Snowy knew their thick ogre hides would heal quickly, but she also knew their anger would last a long time.

Meanwhile, aside from being angered over their injuries, the ogres' enormous bellies were still empty. A collectively loud growling sound reminded the large beasts why they had come to the town in the first place. The ogres slowly began to think the little girls needed to be taught a lesson.

CHAPTER FOUR
PONIES AND TREASURE WAGONS

Minty and Snowy were racing up the hill toward their homes when they came to a screeching halt. The thunderous sound of hoof beats and wagons headed their way. Amid trampling hooves, there was an occasional cracking of a whip, followed by the sound of an ogre yelling orders.

Soon spilling out onto the road from the mountain trail were four wagons, each with a team of four ponies. One giant ogre was driving them all, obviously surprised to see two dainty girls in the road. He brought the wagons to a rumbling stop.

Minty and Snowy weren't so much scared as they were shocked. The ponies were slaves! Thin and frail, it must have been weeks since they had last eaten a good meal.

The ogre driver drooled at the girls. "Food!" he grunted, raising his whip and cracking it at the two friends.

Just as the tail of the whip snapped close to them, Minty and Snowy sprang into cartwheels. They spun like pinwheels in two different directions to distract the ogre, chanting the words they always sang when they played tag in the forest, "Ha-ha! You can't catch me! You can't catch me!"

Again, the ogre's whip cracked in the open air. He seemed unimpressed by the cartwheels. Minty darted off to some bushes at the side of the road, but Snowy was stopped by a furious lash of the whip, snapping right beside her.

With nowhere to go, Snowy darted to the edge of a nearby cliff, overlooking the fast-flowing river below. It was too far down for her to safely dive, so she had to think fast. The ogre had jumped from the wagon and was closing in on her. She was trapped between him and the cliff's edge.

With a snarl, the ogre said in a booming grunt, "Can't catch me, huh?" He laughed and snorted with glee. "I catch you! I hungry!" The ogre opened his mouth and growled at

Snowy, showing large teeth, sharp as daggers and large like a hippo's.

He thudded toward her. The ogre's clammy hands reached so close! Snowy could even smell his stinky breath. He reeked of moldy bread and sour milk. Snowy pinched her nostrils in disgust. Then, she saw something out of the corner of her eye.

Snowy took a deep breath and did the only thing she could think to do. She stuck out her cherry-red tongue and set her hands on her hips. The ogre was outraged at Snowy's sassy actions and pulled back his arm to take a swat at her. At that very moment, Minty burst out of the bushes behind the ogre with her tiny penknife extended. Running into him with all her might, she stuck him squarely in his rear.

The sting of the blade, and the surprise of being pushed, was enough to throw the hairy giant off balance. As he fell forward, Snowy dashed between his giant tree-trunk legs. The ogre tried to grab her as she ran to safety behind him, but it was no use.

Minty snatched up his dropped whip, and a key ring that dangled off his dirty pants. "Yes!" she squealed in victory.

The moist, mossy ground near the edge of the cliff gave way under the heavy weight of the ogre, and with a bark-

like scream, he scrambled to grab hold of something. With a final yell, he slipped over the edge with a tumble of moss, mud, and rocks. Minty and Snowy beamed as they heard the ogre splash into the water below.

"Whew! That was a close one," Snowy gasped, catching her breath. "Bet he won't be causing us any more trouble!"

Gratitude filled her chest with warmth, and she knew what she needed to do. She sank to the ground and covered her face, whispering, "Oh, Lord, thank you for your deliverance. You have allowed two small girls to defeat a giant the likes of Goliath. Thank you, thank you for saving us and our friends!"

Minty gave her best wrinkled-nose smile. "Amen!" she echoed, and extended a hand to her friend.

A neigh from the ponies got their attention, and the girls turned, approaching them with caution. The sweaty slaves were unkempt, underfed, and over-worked. It showed in the shabbiness of their deep gray and black coats. The ponies leaned their heads toward the girls, who stroked their worn muzzles with gentle care and spoke in soft whispers in their ears.

As Minty came close to one pony, it backed away, shivering in fear. Minty realized it was because of the whip she was holding. Her heart clenched as she choked back tears. She tossed the thing into a wagon. "That whip will never touch you again," she said, scratching behind its ears.

To Minty's and Snowy's surprise, two of the wagons were chock full of glistening treasure. There were gold coins, silver chalices, beautiful jeweled necklaces, and a whole lot more! The last two wagons, on the other hand, contained foul-smelling furs that must have been used for the ogre's bedding. Rotten food added to the stench. Lastly, they spotted knotted ropes that had probably been used to hobble the ponies at night.

Without a moment's hesitation, the girls turned and picked some apples from a nearby tree to feed the ponies, who ate voraciously. A more proper meal of hay or grass would have to wait, because Minty heard an ogre yelling in the distance. She and Snowy needed no discussion to know what to do next. As dumb as the ogres were, they would soon figure out their supply wagons had been taken, and come looking for them.

***

Meanwhile, the singed and angry ogres in town had begun recovering from the fireball and sugar surprise. Taking stock, they could see that Krag had been killed by the church bell that had fallen from the bell tower, and the others were in various states of crankiness. In a stupor, they all looked at each other, wondering what they would do without Krag. Eventually, all eyes landed on Booger. He was the smartest of the ogres. He could even read a little, but Booger was scared. He wasn't ready to lead. He was not trained as a leader, and neither was he brave and fearless like Krag. Nonetheless, Badger, the oldest and ugliest of the ogre clan, took Krag's gigantic sword and handed it to Booger. Whether he liked it or not, Booger had become the ogres' new leader.

Booger gave his best snarly look, setting his massive jaw, and took the sword with more fierceness displayed than he actually felt in his heart.

All the ogres, covered in sticky sugar, scowled at the deserted city square, wondering where the girls went. Mog, another of the powerful ogres, pointed to two sets of small, sugary footprints near the side of the church. They continued around to the main road from which the ogres had arrived.

The white footprints were an exciting find. Booger raised his new sword into the air, and yelled, "This way!" With a grunt, trying to keep his voice from cracking in front of the troops, he yelled again.

"Let's go!" he shouted, but since most of the ogres were busy licking the sugar off their hands, they did not notice Booger's quivering voice.

***

Back at the wagons, Minty and Snowy unhooked the one with the rotten ogre food, and used the hobble ropes to tether its team of ponies to the front of one of the treasure wagons. Minty set fire to the wagon with the rotten stench before turning the wagons around. Slowly they drove them up the road away from Epping, eastward toward Maldon. As the three wagons wheeled along the slippery, muddy road, Minty tossed out the putrid furs one by one, to help gain traction.

They approached a steep hill and started to make their way up, but the ponies had a difficult time with the weight of the loaded treasure wagons. Minty looked at Snowy, and Snowy looked at Minty, and they each gave a wink. They had an idea.

***

Meanwhile, Booger could see smoke rising in the distance up the road, and the band of ogres started jogging toward it. As they got closer, they heard a familiar voice yelling for help. It was Barlow, the ogre who was in charge of the wagons, clinging to a boulder in the center of the river. Drenched and shivering, he held on with one hand, and grabbed his stinging rear with the other.

Booger couldn't imagine what had happened to poor Barlow, but he gruffly ordered some of the other ogres to assist him. As they approached the area, they could see that one of their wagons was on fire, and they could smell burning food. Booger's lips quivered with disappointment. Instead of tears though, he mustered up some proper ogre anger and yelled, "They burned our food!"

Booger lifted his sword in the air and ran along the road, following the wagon tracks. The ogres moved quickly, their stomachs growling louder and louder.

Their jog slowed to a trot as the road became steeper. The food in the burning wagon was maggot-infested bread, along with a few squirrels and deer they snatched up on the way to the village. Despite this delicious fare, that morning many had skipped breakfast, thinking they would dine instead on a plump villager or two. As if the hunger pangs were not enough, their treasure wagons had been stolen! Then, a short way up the road came the final straw. In a large mud puddle, in the middle of the road, was Booger's pink blanket!

The band of ogres surrounded Booger as he knelt down and plucked the blanket from the puddle. He thrust his thumb into his mouth, hugging the now muddy security blanket. *At least those nasty little girls did not burn it!*

Booger tried to regain his fierce stance before his fellow ogres, but it was too late. They had seen Booger having a tender moment with his pink blanket, and with disgust, Badger grabbed Krag's sword from Booger's hand. "I leader now!" Badger roared as he pushed him away. The announcement was a huge relief for Booger, who dared not protest.

Minty and Snowy had parked the third empty wagon at the top of a steep hill and tied the ponies to the treasure wagons. On the way back, Snowy spotted a black currant bush on the side of the road. Since they were both hungry, they grabbed a handful of the tart berries for a snack. They were hardly Minty's famous cinnamon buns, but the sour, deep-purple fruit was still welcome.

The girls kept the empty wagon from rolling back down the hill by placing a large branch behind the two rear wagon wheels. Then, by pulling with all their might, they set the driver's hand brake. They had a plan...

As Minty filled the wagon with rocks, Snowy tied the ponies' hobble ropes together to make one very long cord. She tethered one end to the large branch behind the wheels, running the other end down the hill, through the bushes and small trees. It eventually snaked out to the center of the road. Snowy knotted her handkerchief to its end, and with some berry juice, she finger-painted in big lctters thc warning: *DO NOT PULL!*

Snowy peered up the hill to make sure the wagon was hidden well enough by bushes. She soon heard ogres fast approaching, so she scurried back up to her friend as quickly as she could.

Minty had used some long tree branches as levers and ramps, to roll larger rocks into the wagon. As she loaded the last boulder, the wagon creaked in protest over such a heavy load. The girls carefully released the hand brake. At first, it looked as if it would roll away, but the movement actually managed to lodge the branch in further behind the back wheels. The girls tiptoed away.

A short time later and farther up the hill, Minty and Snowy each drove one of the other wagons down the road toward Maldon. Snowy bit her lip in anticipation, while Minty started giggling wildly. Even Galileo the cat suddenly reappeared up in the top of a nearby tree, curiously watching the tumultuous happenings down below.

Badger could hear the horses and wagons in the distance, and so they continued to run toward the hill. With his one good eye, he soon saw the white handkerchief in the middle of the road. The group of ogres gathered around it, breathless. They didn't understand the words written, but their keen sense of smell told them that the little girls had been there.

Badger grabbed the handkerchief, looking at it with his good eye open and the other closed. "Hmm, says something with writing. Booger come read dis." Badger pulled on the rope as he motioned for Booger.

Booger obeyed.

"What it says?" Badger pulled on the rope again, curious as to why the handkerchief was also tied to a piece of rope.

Booger read the words out loud, "*Do not pull.* It says *do not pull!*"

Badger cupped an ear. "I hear rumble."

"Uh-oh," they said in unison.

The wagon was in motion, barreling down the hill toward the burly ogres. Booger frantically jumped out of the way, and just like that, the rumbling cargo collided with Badger and several others. Rocks exploded everywhere, and the wagon cartwheeled into the air. The road became a scramble of rocks, wagon wood, dirt, dazed ogres, and wheels.

When the dust settled from the devastating collision, all were silent, the rag-tag band of ogres shocked. This had been the worst day ever for plundering, and all because of two little girls!

Booger shook off dirt and plucked thorns from his rear. He was standing safely on the hill, in a bush. Having been the only one to escape the mishap, everyone gathered around. Mog stumbled toward him, extending the slightly bent sword. "Looks like you da leader again," he said.

Booger looked at the bruised and battered ogre band and thought to himself, *Oh no! Not me again!*

Despite his misgivings however, he stood taller and accepted the sword from Mog.

Trying to think of something inspiring to say, he yelled out, "If we hurry, we might have fried girls for supper!"

They all roared in agreement, and then the ogres, minus a few, continued climbing up the road from whence the wagon had come. They were determined to find those pesky little girls.

CHAPTER FIVE
THE CAPTAIN'S SECRET PLAN

Minty and Snowy were making good time in escaping the ogres. The now well-fed slave ponies had plenty of energy, and once the girls had figured out how to hitch two teams to each wagon, their burden was much lighter. The girls could see a river in the distance and a great expanse of blue on the horizon. They would be in Maldon by the afternoon. They hoped to lose the ogres completely by then. Maldon was a big place—not even ogres could fight that many people.

"If we rent a ship," Snowy said, "we can sail around the Southminster Peninsula of England, and meet with the townspeople of Epping in Southend-on-Sea. Maybe then we can call in the army to deal with these ogres properly."

"And take a bath?" Minty replied with hope shimmering in her green eyes. She was busy tying up her long brown hair with a ribbon and a cinnamon stick she had in her pocket. "I fear that I smell like ogre breath by now!"

"Yes, of course, a hot bath and a hot meal for both of us!" Snowy laughed. "With hot tea and pie, and some clean clothes, to boot! Not to mention shoes. I promise, Minty." She glanced down at her sore feet and wiggled her dirty toes—mud flaked off as she did so. It had been a rough day for sure.

Minty and Snowy had never been to Maldon, but they liked it already, simply for the comforts they knew it would bring.

In the distance, large sailing ships floated offshore, bobbing on the high tide. The docks were alive with rigging and cranes, moving crates on and off of various ships. Minty had read many stories of schooners and clipper ships on exciting mid-sea adventures. Exhaustion quickly gave way to excitement, and the girls quickened the ponies' pace.

The road turned from mud to light gravel, and finally cobblestone, as they entered the outskirts of Maldon. They soon came upon a guard shack, low walls extending on either side. They were reinforced with stone and sharp spikes to frighten away those who would do the city harm. Currently however, a thick wooden gate was open, allowing travelers to pass through.

Minty and Snowy stopped to alert the guards about what had happened in Epping. The ogres were mad and probably on their way to Maldon.

The guards looked at the two girls as though they were nothing but silly children making up stories. They didn't even pretend to care. Frustrated, Minty went to the back of the wagon and pulled out a handful of gold pieces. With a greedy glint in their eyes, the guards grudgingly agreed to pay extra close attention for the next few hours.

Minty and Snowy continued on, but looked back in time to see the heavy gate closing. Snowy sighed in relief, entering the protection of the city. They moved with care along the crowded market streets, asking for directions about where to find a ship and crew for hire. The townspeople were friendly, but visibly confused.

Eventually, they were directed to the harbor master's office, and from there, they were directed to a ship called the *Gillfish*. The captain in charge of the *Gillfish* was a certain Mr. Rayer.

After a short conversation upon previewing a bit of the girls' cargo, the dapper-coated Captain Rayer agreed to take Minty and Snowy to Southend-on-Sea in exchange for a reasonable share of their hoard. It was a short voyage, he assured with a tip of his white captain's hat. They would load up the two wagons and all of the ponies immediately, and set sail with the tide that evening. Paying with a fistful of the treasure, Minty completed the negotiations.

Snowy then hired some stable boys to care for the ponies. She ordered that they give them the best food possible before their voyage, and gave detailed instructions for brushing the special animal companions. The boys also took care of Galileo, though Galileo seemed quite certain he could take care of himself without any help.

Several of the guards coming off duty at the town's entrance offered to stand watch over the wagons, ensuring they were loaded on the ship safely—for a small fee, of course.

Minty and Snowy were tired and dirty after the day's events, and resolved to take a bath to get ready for their night at sea. They accepted a few apples and a bit of cheese from the cook, a tall, whiskered fellow with a thick accent and jaunty red kerchief.

Within a few hours, the girls were properly fed, cleaned up with a bath, in possession of shoes and stockings, and ready for a tour of the ship. Once the ponies were properly brushed and fed they were taken below deck for the night.

The wagons were on the center deck, secured with several ropes. The crew was ready to set sail upon Captain Rayer's orders.

Snowy couldn't help herself. She went from crewman to crewman, watched them work, and asked as many questions as she could about how everything worked, until they grew weary of her, sending her away.

As they left the dock and set sail, Minty took a position near the wheel next to the helmsman, where she waited impatiently to take a turn at steering. Eventually, after Minty stood tapping her foot for some time, the helmsman reluctantly turned the wheel over to her. They made their way out of the harbor area and into the open sea just as the sun was beginning to set, the coastline slowly fading away.

After both girls had taken a turn at the wheel, they realized how exhausted they were and retired to their quarters. The gentle rock of the boat was so calming to Minty she felt she must have been born on a ship, and fell right to sleep. It took Snowy a bit longer to get her sea legs. Galileo crept out of the bag where he had been hiding, up to his usual spot, purring atop Snowy's ankles. Only then did Snowy fall into a deep sleep.

In the middle of the night, Minty got up for a drink of water. Yawning and wrapping a scratchy blanket around her shoulders, she pushed open the cabin door and stepped into the hall. The light from the captain's cabin was shining like a sliver of moonlight under his doorway.

She crept across the cold, top deck of the ship, looking up in awe at the twinkling stars. It was as though the ship was sailing right through the galaxy.

Snowy would love to see this, but she needs her sleep, Minty thought with a smile, continuing on.

The helmsman had lashed himself to the wheel with a rope to keep it steady, dozing off while standing there. Minty reached the barrel of drinking water that was set out nearby, and ladled a cup of fresh, cold water.

Minty gulped the contents thirstily, and was almost back to her own cabin door when curiosity about the captain's late hours finally got the best of her. She approached the cabin door with stealth, and listened to the deep voices coming from the other side.

She peeked through a knothole in the wooden door. The light inside the room was bright, and she could see two figures, one of which was Captain Rayer. The other was a dark man, who was tall and muscular. She could not see the tall man's face, but the depth of his voice sent a chill down her spine. Pressing her ear closer to the door, Minty listened to their conversation.

"Then it's settled," the deep voice said. "At first light, I'll bring my ship in from the fog and surprise your ship. You will be ready with the fake wooden cannonballs and give a valiant show of defense, but in the end you will be overwhelmed by the power of my ship.

"Then we'll board the *Gillfish*, and you'll plead for the lives of your crew, and the girls', in exchange for the treasure. We'll take the treasure aboard the *Fog* and sail away. When you drop off your passengers in Southend, we can meet up and split the treasure sixty—"

Just then, a forceful wave hit the ship. Minty reached out her hand to the wall to brace herself. She was half-paralyzed from what she had just heard! She accidentally bumped the stand that held a signal lantern, and it fell to the deck with a loud crash. The fuel inside the lamp burst into flames.

Minty darted around the flames toward the front of the ship, not knowing that a lock of her hair had been singed by a drop of flaming lamp oil. She raced past the masts and into the dark passageway of the forward cabin entrance. From the darkness, she watched the deep-voiced man exit the captain's cabin.

The stranger must have stood seven feet tall with gray hair extending down from underneath his three-cornered hat. When the flames lit his features, Minty could see that he had scars on one side of his face, and underneath his black overcoat, he wore a dark red vest with large gold buttons.

The man looked left and right, eyeing the lantern's flames, wondering how it had been knocked off the stand. Then, with supernatural force, he blew an icy breath extinguishing the fire all at once.

In amazement, Minty continued to watch as Captain Rayer joined the man. Rayer looked over at the groggy helmsman and asked, "What's going on here?"

The helmsman was as surprised and confused as Captain Rayer. When the captain's gaze began sweeping across the deck, Minty knew she had better retreat to her cabin. No sooner had she put her head on the pillow than she heard the footsteps of Captain Rayer's enormous rubber boots on the deck, squeaking toward her cabin. Quietly, the girls' cabin door creaked open. Minty stiffened and peeked over at Snowy, who was out cold. Minty closed her eyes and tried to slow her anxious breathing, pretending to be asleep.

Without hearing a sound for several minutes, Minty eventually heard the door creak to a close. However, when she should have heard footsteps walking away, she heard silence. She kept her head down, breathing deep.

Meanwhile, Captain Rayer was waiting outside the door for any sound. His suspicion was piqued, because he swore he smelled singed hair in the girls' cabin. So he walked in place, pretending to have left, before listening some more.

Minty didn't budge. She remembered the games of hide-and-seek with her older brother, and she wasn't about to take that bait.

Finally, Captain Rayer turned and walked away, mumbling that even if they knew what was going on, there was certainly nothing that two little girls could do about it. Plus, he needed to go punish that lazy helmsman for sleeping on the job.

CHAPTER SIX
BATTLE AT SEA

Sunlight was just peeking through the cabin window when Minty heard yelling.

"What? Oh no! I actually fell asleep!" she gasped.

She threw back the covers and saw that Snowy was already out of bed, and was nowhere in sight. Memories of last night came flooding back. It was now too late to warn anyone, or come up with a plan. By the sounds she heard, they were already under attack!

Minty scrambled out of bed and dashed up the stairs, every step echoing against the wood walls of the ship. The deck was alive with sailors running about like frantic ants, making ready for a battle at sea. They pulled the cannons that were on the main deck to the starboard side. An unnatural wall of fog was heading straight toward them, the outline of a huge, dark ship barely visible in its depths.

"Oh no!" she gasped. "What I heard is really happening!" She felt her face go hot and tears threatened to fall from her eyes.

Minty bolted to Snowy, who was at the helm with the captain and first mate. Both girls began speaking at once. Minty pulled Snowy aside and interrupted her questions to tell her the plans she had overheard the night before.

Meanwhile, some sailors were bringing gunpowder to the main deck, while others pulled ropes to open the doors to the gunnery deck. Captain Rayer was obviously pretending not to watch them talk. peeking at them as he glanced back at the first mate, who was focused on getting the men ready for action.

Whispering into Snowy's ear, Minty explained, "I know this sounds crazy, but I need you to set the ponies free, and we need to replace those fake cannonballs with real ones." Minty pointed to a tray of cannonballs that were being rolled out.

With that, Minty looked at Snowy, and Snowy looked at Minty. They each gave a wink. The girls burst into action. Snowy ran below the deck to get the ponies. Minty ran back to her cabin, grabbed the ogre's hateful whip, and slipped her lucky penknife into her pocket. She also shut Galileo safely inside the tiny room before running back toward the helm.

As she reached the helm, a black pirate ship emerged from the foggy cloud and began to turn its side to the *Gillfish.* Everyone could clearly see it as the doors to the gunnery deck were slowly lifted in preparation to fire.

Just then came loud neighs from below. Several ponies jumped through the open passageway onto the main deck with a clatter of skittish hooves on slippery wood. It was confusing to everyone, the ponies' eyes wide, sensing the stress of the situation.

Captain Rayer yelled to his first mate, a young man. "Carter, take care of those mangy animals!"

Carter immediately moved toward the ponies. Minty handed him the whip, and said, "You'll need this!"

Three more ponies jumped onto the deck from below. From the yelling on the gunnery deck, everyone knew that more were there too.

Minty said to Captain Rayer, "We'll just be getting out of your way, sir," as she jumped down onto the main deck.

The main deck buzzed with activity as the sailors tried to grab the ponies. The frightened creatures were wild, running and rearing up on their hind legs.

Minty heard a familiar birdlike whistle, and ran, dodging horses and sailors, to where Snowy was waiting. Snowy had found the hold where the real cannonballs were kept.

Minty and Snowy put all of their might into carrying real cannonballs onto the top deck, switching out the wooden ones one by one. Fortunately, they went unnoticed amid all the chaos.

First Mate Carter cracked the whip over the ponies' heads, and it was as if the world went silent at the sound. In that moment, all of the ponies stopped what they were doing, focusing their attention on the weapon, immediately snapping from skittish to angry. They had been abused by that whip when it belonged to the ogres, and the little horses were not going to let that happen again!

The largest of the ponies, one Snowy had named Shadow, lowered his head and rushed at Carter with fierce determination in his eyes. Carter was immediately knocked off balance, hitting the deck.

Suddenly, the other ponies jumped around and kicked, bucked, and pushed at everything that moved. It was such pandemonium that the dark pirate ship did not fire, all hands busy watching the craziness aboard the *Gillfish.*

As Carter stood and lifted the whip again, Shadow kicked him hard. He flew head over heels through the air, landing hard on the deck, sliding into a pile of ropes.

Snowy and Minty took full advantage of the confusion. They hustled below to the gunnery deck, exchanging the fake cannonballs there, too.

The girls' hearts jumped in their chests as a sudden whistle of cannonballs, and the percussion of their impact, interrupted things. The dark ship had finally opened fire on the *Gillfish*. Not too far from where Minty and Snowy stood, one of the balls slammed into the side of the ship with a frightening crash. Splinters of wood flew through the air. Despite the explosion, however, damage was minimal because they were launching wooden cannonballs.

Snowy checked to make sure all the *Gillfish's* fake cannonballs had been replaced, while Minty ran back to the top deck. Minty saw the frightened ponies were now scrambling toward the back of the ship. One of the older sailors was using his hat to shoo the frightened animals toward the opening leading below deck. Minty was happy to see them willingly trotting away from the chaos, back down to safety.

Minty ran to the main mast, and started to climb up its rope ladder.

"Men, get to your guns!" Minty shouted.

Captain Rayer looked down from the command deck upon his crew in consternation. "Yes, fire men. FIRE!"

When the real cannonballs were launched, the blast was much deeper, the impact much more powerful. Gunpowder temporarily obscured everyone's view. Below deck, more guns fired, and Snowy grabbed one of the rammers to help reload the cannons there.

"Faster, men, faster!" yelled Snowy. "Give 'em two for every one they fire at us!"

Minty had climbed about halfway up the mast when she saw what she was looking for—a rope hanging down that would be just right.

Captain Rayer watched Minty, but then looked over at the dark pirate ship in terror. The cannonballs had a devastating effect! Large holes now gaped in the side of the vessel, and one of the forward masts had cracked.

"Oh no!" he said, watching the mast completely topple, its sails collapsing. "Captain Savage will kill me for this!"

Minty jumped for the rope, and swung gracefully through the air toward Captain Rayer. He was busy raising his arms, frantically yelling at his men to stop.

"Yoo-hoo!" Minty called, lifting her legs straight out in front of her. Before the captain knew what was happening, she crashed into him and caught him completely by surprise. His hat flew off his head as he was thrown over the side of the ship into the cold seawater below.

Minty regained her footing, snatched up the captain's hat, and yelled fiercely, "What are you men looking at? FIRE!" With that, the next round of real cannonballs took flight.

Minty continued barking orders, and such was her authority that the sailors obeyed. The pirate ship took several more hits, igniting a fire aboard. Minty dared to hope that its evil captain would soon go down with his ship.

Snowy stayed below deck, helping to reload cannons, and encouraging the sailors. "Come on, men! You can do this. You must defend your ship! Let's give these pirates a serious case of lead poisoning!"

With Snowy's help, the crew continued firing one cannon after another. The pirate ship soon turned sharply in the water, away from the *Gillfish*. Minty ordered the *Gillfish* crew to turn also, attempting to stay broadside.

As another round of cannon fire erupted from the *Gillfish*, the pirate ship fired back. Minty saw they too were now using real cannonballs. The dark spheres hit with frightening force, ripping into the deck.

Minty called off the attack. The flaming pirate ship turned away from the *Gillfish,* and into a wall of fog.

The stunned crew of the *Gillfish* watched in silence for a couple minutes, and then cheered with joy. They had faced the dreaded Captain Savage and his ship, the *Fog,* and lived!

Snowy ran up the stairs to see her best friend. Minty stood on the command deck beaming with pride at her first naval victory. The excited crew cheered some more in celebration.

"But what happened to Captain Rayer?" Snowy asked.

The crew members pointed to the water. Snowy peered over the side, down at Captain Rayer. He was swimming with all his might, trying to stay afloat, but before anyone could drop him a rope to oblige his efforts, Minty got the crew's attention with a strong clap of her small hands.

"Men," she said. "Who among you knew that Captain Rayer was in league with that pirate, in order to steal our treasure?"

The men were confused, and though some of them whispered to their neighbor, none responded to Minty's question. So Minty recounted what she had heard and seen the night before.

"How do we know you're telling the truth?" one sailor asked with an arrogant sneer.

"You'll see..." Minty jumped down to the main deck, disappearing with Snowy soon at her side.

A few minutes later, the girls emerged with a tray of cannonballs held between them. One of the sailors nudged another saying, "Those girls are pretty strong!"

"You see, men," Minty said. "Captain Rayer was in on this trick. We can tell by the way he replaced real cannonballs with these fake wooden ones. He didn't really want to damage the pirate ship."

The girls flung the fake cannonballs over the edge of the ship, close to where Captain Rayer was still treading. The crew looked on in silence as each of the balls disappeared under the water and bobbed right back up.

The oldest sailor, Mr. Clements, approached Minty. "I'm sorry, Miss, what is your name?" he asked.

"Minty is my name," she replied with bravado.

Mr. Clements turned to the other sailors. "Hurray for Captain Minty! She has earned our respect with her brave deeds!"

The men cheered with enthusiasm. One of the sailors took the captain's coat from Mr. Rayer's cabin and wrapped her in it. "You are the best Captain a ship could have!" he shouted.

Mr. Clements spoke for the entire crew. "Captain Minty, if you will have us, we will be your crew and this will be your ship. We will serve you faithfully for all of your days."

Minty smiled and agreed with a wink. She was immediately swept up by the crew, and paraded around the deck to all sorts of cheers and hollering.

Snowy was very proud of her new captain friend, and laughed thinking it might be difficult to get Minty's ship all the way inland to Epping Forest.

First Mate Carter was just waking from being knocked out cold, when some sailors updated him on everything that had happened. Although amazed at Minty's bravery, he too was elated. Suddenly the crew wanted to dance and sing some old nautical songs.

Minty had no time to really celebrate, and besides that, the crew's attention became a bit overwhelming. "All right, men," she laughed, blushing. "Great job sending those pirates packing, but we need to get this ship fixed and to port. So let's get to work!"

Snowy looked over the side of the ship to see Captain Rayer swimming toward the fog, where the pirate ship had disappeared.

CHAPTER SEVEN
CAPTAIN MINTY GOES TO SOUTHEND-ON-SEA

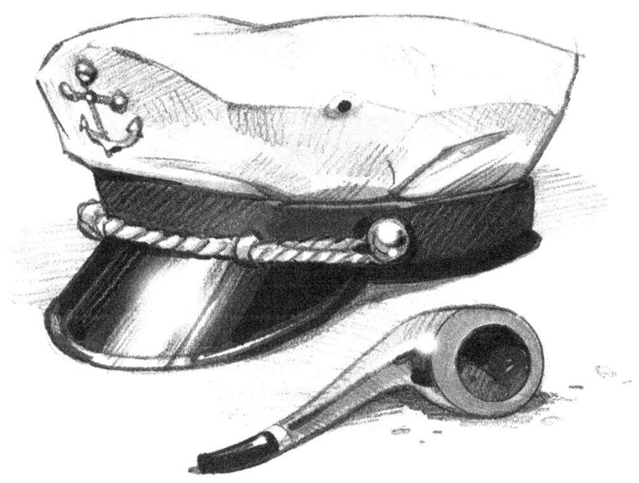

The *Gillfish* sailed into port at Southend-on-Sea with Minty at the wheel. Under the advice of the helmsman, she steered the ship to the end of the wharf where there was an open berth, and the crew prepared to unload for repairs.

It was midday, but not a soul at port stirred. The ship's crew was unnerved by the strangely quiet and empty streets. It was usually crowded with people bustling about their business.

"What do we do, Captain?" Mr. Clements asked. "There doesn't seem to be a single person here. What are your orders, sir? Um, I mean, *miss.*"

"Hmm..." Minty hesitated. "Men, please get the wagons ready to unload. We'll send a small group out to find out what's going on. They will report back to us as soon as they can. In the meantime, please make repairs, and post a watch and guard. We may need to set sail at a moment's notice."

"And please take care of my cat!" Snowy shouted from across the ship.

The men understood Minty's clear orders and set about making them so. She, Snowy, First Mate Carter, and Sailor Shepard—whose hometown was Southend—climbed down the gangplank.

Sailor Shepard helped navigate the unfamiliar streets. He mentioned how strange it was to see the harbor's storefronts empty on what should have been a busy shopping day.

As they walked, they saw something else very peculiar, golden goo. It was smeared and dripping down rooftops and lamp posts, storefronts and street signs.

Minty inspected a hardened dollop of goo that clung to a fence post. She knocked on it, but it didn't budge. She pulled out her penknife, and with great effort she was able to break off a small piece. It had a distinct floral smell, tangy-sweet like honey.

The others watched as she continued to examine the clump in her hand. They knew what she was doing must be important, but had no idea why.

Minty finally put the mystery clump in her pocket, and the group went on into the heart of the port town. They saw more golden clusters sticking to the edges of various homes.

Like everywhere else, the town center was empty of people. It was so quiet they could still hear ringing in their ears from the cannon's firing. Most windows and doors were left open, so the crew warily peeked inside a few houses.

All the kitchens appeared to have been ransacked. Cupboards were bare, their doors hanging on bent and broken hinges. In one home, Snowy lifted the lid of a pot that hung over a burnt-out fire pit. The stew inside had gone bad, topped with a thin layer of fuzzy white mold. Southend must have been abandoned sometime within the past two or three days.

"I wonder why they took all the food, except for what was in the pot?" Minty asked, with a raised eyebrow. "Perhaps whomever or whatever did this is afraid of fire?"

The group continued to search through the town, when Snowy noticed something in the distant sky—smoke rising from a chimney.

They walked in the direction of the smoke. The sun was just starting to set, and there was an uncomfortable chill in the air. The streets stayed desolate, lonely. No matter how softly they treaded, their footsteps along the cobblestones echoed.

As they approached the large building with the chimney, they could smell fresh baked bread, yeasty rolls, and sweets, like mince pies and chocolate cake. The girls, Mr. Shepard, and First Mate Carter were very hungry, and the smells they could almost taste only made them hungrier.

Snowy thought fondly of Minty's cinnamon buns, pastries, and piping hot chamomile tea. The thought gave her a pang of homesickness, missing all the wonderful little things she loved about being at home.

As they approached the bakery, smoke from the wood ovens swirled out and around the street, climbing up buildings and misting through open windows. They noticed there was dramatically less amber-colored residue here near the bakery than at the harbor. A sign read, *Sneezie's Pastries and Bakery*. They listened at the door. Someone inside was making an awful racket, clanging pots and pans, and humming off-tune.

CHAPTER EIGHT
GREEN TREATS

Minty cautiously opened the door of the bakery to peek inside. She saw towering stacks of fine pastries, beautifully decorated wedding cakes, sugar-sprinkled muffins, breads of different shapes, and thousands of cookies—every kind, from chocolate chip to oatmeal, and shortbread to buttery gingersnaps. "Mmmm," was all she could say.

At that, Snowy peeked over Minty's shoulder. The girls' hungry stomachs drove them inside, a bell ringing in merry chimes upon their entering. A plump baker was working with earnest precision to frost a giant purple cake. Then Sneezie, as they assumed him to be, looked up at them with surprise. "Oh dear... Hello!" he said in a very nasally voice.

The girls nodded, waiting to hear if Sneezie would welcome them. "Hello," they said in unison.

"I'm so glad someone else is here! Everyone in Southend has been gone for days. Come in, come in, please." Sneezie motioned to Mr. Shepard and First Mate Carter who stood in the doorway. "Please come in and help yourself to any baked goods that catch your fancy."

Minty and Snowy each grabbed molasses cookies studded with raisins and small chunks of chocolate. "What happened to everyone?" they asked, just before taking a bite.

"Well, that's a long story, but let me start from the very beginning." Sneezie grabbed a big mixing bowl and cracked an egg into it. "Several weeks back, we started to see these strange bees flying around town. They were huge—some the size of dogs. At first, there was little worry, as they seemed to be scared of people. They'd fly away as soon as anyone got near them."

Everyone grabbed another cookie as Sneezie cracked a few more eggs into the bowl, dropped in some sugar, and stirred the mixture vigorously. As Sneezie worked, Snowy noticed that his nose was running, and he sniffed before he continued with his story.

"The townsfolk didn't think much of it, but a few days later, the bees came back. This time, they were in a swarm.

The bees flew all around the town, and everyone was concerned about how great they were in number, and the way they buzzed about everywhere."

As Sneezie continued stirring the ingredients, Snowy and Minty noticed that drips from his runny nose were dropping into the batter. Snowy, Minty, Mr. Shepard, and First Mate Carter froze in mid-chew, trying not to think about what they had already eaten.

Sneezie added, "The swarm didn't land very often, but people were panicked and asked the mayor and city council what they should do. They called a town meeting and everyone gathered at the town hall. While they were meeting, a stranger came and introduced himself. His name was Pontius Pilate, and he said he was the owner of a pest control company that had just opened on the outskirts of town, where... *Ahchoo!*" Sneezie suddenly, and violently, sneezed. A fine spray covered the counter top, cake batter, utensils, and baking sheets. It fell just short of reaching the petrified visitors.

Sneezie looked at his observers with sheepish eyes. "Excuse me, I've been sick for several weeks now, and I just can't seem to shake it!" The baker used his green apron to wipe his nose.

Minty reluctantly swallowed the bit of cookie that lingered in her mouth. Her stomach churned in protest.

"Yes, his name was Pontius Pilate," continued Sneezie, "and he ran Pontius Pilate Pest Control. He said that Southend had a glue bee problem, and that if not dealt with very soon, the entire town would be destroyed by glue bees. He talked about how he had seen them before in Asia, and that they were fiercely strong bees, more than a match for ordinary people. He said that one sting from a glue bee could kill a grown man! Imagine! But even worse than that was the glue bee honey they'd leave behind. He said the bees would place glue honey everywhere, and when someone got stuck in it, the bees would know, and they'd come to swarm around the stuck person. *Ahchoo!*"

Another sneeze made everyone cringe again. This one was so forceful that it blew a cloud of flour out of a bowl and into the air.

Peering through the cloud, Sneezie resumed baking, as he took the batter he had been mixing and poured it into a pan lined with parchment paper. "Pontius Pilate said that whoever got stuck in the glue honey would surely be eaten alive by the bees, and that only his special power over the bees could rid the town of them. He also said that it would cost the city thirty pieces of silver for each and every day that he kept the bees away. The town council couldn't believe what they heard. Some thought Pontius Pilate must be a crook, and others thought that everyone should listen and do whatever he suggested.

"Pontius left the town council meeting. Within an hour, more bees swarmed into town. This time the bees left their honey glue wherever they landed. The townspeople were scared, especially when they touched the honey and it was sticky, hardening to an unbreakable, solid material within minutes.

"The next day was even worse. Thousands of bees flew all around the town, depositing honey glue on everything imaginable. They got into people's homes and ruined people's belongings. They grabbed all the food in sight, leaving villagers with no food to feed their children."

Sneezie snorted up some drips, and wiped his nose on the other corner of his apron. The onlookers' stomachs heaved.

Abruptly, the baker turned from his batter. He loaded a rubber spatula with pink frosting, and slathered it on a cooled cake as he spun it on a decorator's wheel. With the expertise of an extraordinary artist, he swirled the frosting here and there, as though working with a magic wand, beautifully dressing the cake in color.

"The town council called an emergency meeting and voted to pay Pontius the thirty pieces of silver he had asked for to keep the bees away. Each day after that, Pontius stood on the edge of town and played his flute, while all the glue bees that were in the area flew off in haste. This went on for several weeks.

"Each day a messenger was sent to Pontius' warehouse to pay him thirty pieces of silver. The townspeople felt safe as long as they could count on Pontius to take the glue bees away when they swarmed the town. Then one day..." Sneezie lowered his raspy voice and spoke in a mysterious tone as he continued, "one day one of the messengers went to the warehouse earlier than usual to make the payment. The messenger peeked through a crack in one wall and saw that Pontius was talking to one of the bees and telling them what to do! He was training the bees! He was their *master*!

"So, with that news, of course the town council was outraged and sent a group of men to arrest Pontius and bring him to the town square. When the men got to his warehouse however, Pontius began to play his magic flute.

Just then, Sneezie let out a huge sneeze, and a large chunk of something flew out of his nose. Minty leaned to the side just in time, and the chunk landed squarely on the cookie in her hand. She gulped back a gag and put the cookie down on the counter. She wiped her hands on her skirt until her fingers began to chafe against the fabric.

Without missing a beat, Sneezie continued his story. "The men were captivated by the flute music. They disappeared into Pontius' warehouse. Shortly afterward, the bees were back in town and swarmed the people again. This time, they stole absolutely every morsel of food from everyone's home, and more importantly, the bees carried off everything of value, too. Silver, gold, you name it and they took it! They scared everyone, but they stayed away from my bakery. I think it's because they don't like the wood smoke."

Sneezie seemed rather proud of his accomplishment and beamed, his eyes twinkling over his red, bulbous nose. He excused himself to blow his nose vigorously into a washcloth. Minty and Snowy felt even queasier. They could hardly handle more snot. They looked up at the men and saw that they, too, were sickened.

"For some reason, since I've been sick, nobody in town has wanted to buy any pastries or bread from me, so business has been very slow, even before everyone disappeared.

"Anyway, Pontius marched straight into town playing his flute, and whoever heard it seemed to be under his spell. They marched with him, completely captivated! I even started to follow him, but my ears became so clogged up that eventually I couldn't hear him anymore.

"So I snuck back to my bakery and wasn't sure what to do. I checked around town, and I'm the only one left. I've been baking non-stop ever since, but there's no one to eat the goodies. Have a marzipan plum?" Sneezie gestured towards the marzipan display with the same washcloth on which he had blown his nose, and then tidily wiped off the counter.

That was all Snowy could take. She darted out of the bakery, quite ill. Minty fared a little better, managing a polite goodbye.

"Well, Sneezie," she said as she backed away toward the door, "You stay here and keep perfecting your baking skills. We will see what we can do to get the townspeople back."

Sneezie nodded and smiled. He pulled a batch of cookies out of the oven before sneezing all over them.

Minty, Mr. Shepard, and First Mate Carter left, declining as politely as possible Sneezie's offers of mint truffles, cranberry shortbread, and a pineapple trifle that looked delicious, but highly suspicious with bits of yellow-green mixed in the layers.

Once outside, Minty looked at Snowy, and Snowy looked at Minty, and they both stuck out their tongues in disgust.

"I hope we don't get sick," said Minty.

Snowy gave a funny look. "What did you say?" she asked. "My ears are all stuffy. I can't hear what you said."

She shook her head from side to side, gently smacking an ear.

"Oh no!" exclaimed Minty.

Mr. Shepard reached into his pocket, grabbed a handkerchief, and blew his nose. First Mate Carter started to sniff.

"'Oh no' is right! We're all gonna get sick!" Snowy moaned.

CHAPTER NINE
PONTIUS PILATE

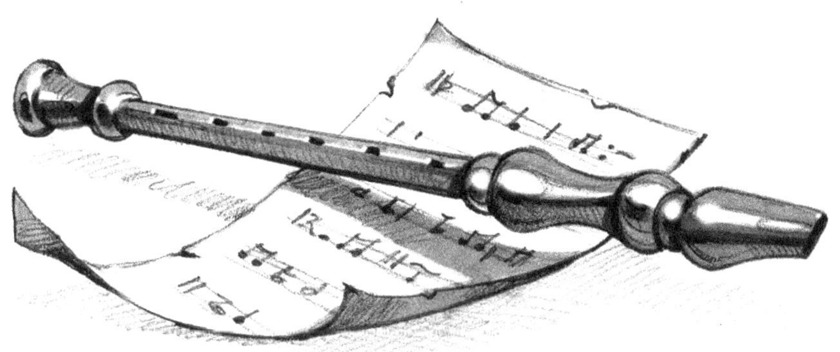

As the tired group stood outside of Sneezie's bakery shop, in the late evening, even in the dim light they could see each other's faces and knew that Sneezie had shared his illness with each of them. "Don't think about it. Mind over matter!" Snowy took the situation in stride and tried to encourage the others.

She put her hands on her hips in her best imitation of a leader, though she would have liked nothing more than to be in her cozy bed, drinking hot broth and resting. Always the trooper however, she said, "I have an idea. Perhaps we can bribe Pontius to release the townspeople if we give him the treasure wagons!"

"Hmm, maybe that would work!" Minty said. "Once we get the townspeople free, we can figure out how to get the treasure back."

Looking to the first mate, Minty said, "Can you get back to the ship and get the wagons unloaded? We will need them.

"But before we do that, we need to cover each man's ears"—Minty paused to sneeze— "with cotton balls, and then have a group stand ready with weapons, as we may need them."

With that, Minty and Snowy headed to the town square alone, while Mr. Shepard and First Mate Carter headed to the ship.

The girls felt weak and tired, so they walked slowly but steadily. "We're almost there," encouraged Snowy. "Let's just keep putting one foot in front of the other until we make it. That's all we have to do."

Once they made it to the town square, their first stop was the community well. Minty turned the handle and the bucket rose slowly from below. The girls took turns drinking the cool, refreshing water.

Her mouth positioned below the bucket, Snowy tipped it some more. Instead of water, a small crab fell out onto her face! She was so surprised by the creature, she instantly dropped the bucket and crab back into the well. "What in the world was that?" she gasped.

"It was a crab. How bizarre!" Minty laughed, but it sounded more like a snort because her throat was scratchy and sore.

"It was *not* funny!" Snowy said with a smile, unable to hold back a giggle.

In the distance came a clatter of hooves and wagon wheels on cobblestone. As the wagons approached, Snowy noted that First Mate Carter and three other men were armed with crossbows, their ears stuffed with cotton balls. Snowy was glad to see them, but Minty looked too sick and tired to care. Her face was pale and her eyes were bloodshot.

"Minty, why don't you stay here and get some rest?" Snowy suggested, putting a hand on her shoulder. "There is no need for you to go along."

Surprisingly, Minty agreed. She unhitched one of the ponies and rode it back to the ship so she could rest. With the treasure wagons, Snowy, First Mate Carter, and the other crewmen headed to the warehouse of Pontius Pilate's Pest Control.

The road eventually transitioned from cobblestone to dirt. As they left the town behind, houses became fewer and farther between, until Snowy and company could see only the massive warehouse at the end of the road. A large sign above the main entrance's huge sliding door said *Pontius Pilate's Pest Control* in big, bold, red letters.

The wagons halted out front, and Snowy motioned for two men to go to either side of the sliding doors. The plan was to keep their ears covered while waiting for her signal to load crossbows for action.

First Snowy stepped down from the wagon and paused to blow her nose with a handkerchief. Again came the thought of her cozy bed. She felt worse, but knew she needed to continue her rescue mission. After all, there was a town to save.

From the treasure wagon, she grabbed a heavy golden candelabra and bag of silver. She approached the large sliding doors. The men on each side of the door crouched down, disappearing into the shadows.

Snowy slammed the bag into the door, making a crude knock. She waited with great patience, putting her ear to the door to listen for someone approaching from the other side. Her ears were so clogged, of course, that she could not hear a thing.

Suddenly, the doors opened, and before her stood a tall man wearing green pants and a darker green shirt. His tan hat had a long green feather in it, and his mouth held a smoldering cigar.

"What do you want?" the man said, glaring, clearly annoyed at the sight of a little girl disturbing him. Snowy could tell that he was one of those unfortunate grownups who assume that children do not have anything important to say or add to the world.

"My name is Snowy," she said proudly. "I would like to pay for the release of all the people of Southend-on-Sea. And...for you to never charm them again!"

With a puzzled look on his face, the man simply continued to glare, finally asking, "What did you say?"

Snowy continued patiently, "You see, I have this silver and this candelabra." She tossed the silver at Pontius' feet.

Pontius looked at her. "It will take much more than that to free the entire town," he scoffed, and took a long draw from his stinky cigar. He blew smoke in Snowy's face with a taunting look in his eyes.

"Fine!" Snowy coughed and walked over to the back of one of the wagons. She pulled down the gate. A pile of gold, gems and other treasures poured out onto the ground. "Would that do it?" she asked.

Pontius Pilate came over, obviously surprised, staring at the pile of treasure. A last coin clinked to the ground as Snowy gave what she hoped looked like a casual shrug, waving his offending cigar smoke away.

Pontius smirked and reached into his shirt pocket to pull out a small flute. "Ah! Now you seem like a smart enough child," he paused, grinning, "but what's to stop me, little brat, from putting you under my spell like all the rest, and simply taking the treasure?"

He started to blow an entrancing melody on his flute, but she could barely hear it because of her ears being so clogged. He played more. She stood, arms crossed, defiant.

"Come on, now," Snowy teased, suddenly waving her arms like a symphony conductor. "You can keep better timing than that! I do believe you were a bit sharp on that last C note!"

Pontius glared at her, playing louder.

Snowy giggled. "And didn't you know that smoking is bad for your lungs? It won't be long before you won't even be able to blow air through that thing!"

Pontius' smirk changed to a look of irritation. He stomped his foot, playing faster.

"Oh, and by the way, if you haven't noticed, I'm immune to your powers." Snowy was really tired by now, and a little cross, her mood evident in her voice. "So do we have a deal, or what?"

With a motion of her fingers, the two archers emerged from the shadows to either side of Pontius.

Pontius stopped playing the flute. His eyebrows raised at the four cocked crossbows pointing at him. "Yes," he finally drawled, "I'll release the townspeople in exchange for the wagon load of treasure.

"Perhaps I *was* a bit hasty. It does seem like a fair trade," he added, though finishing under his breath, "you little brat!"

Piping one last melody, Pontius broke the spell over the townspeople.

With that, the men lowered their crossbows, and Snowy rushed into the warehouse. She soon returned with the townspeople in tow and stopped to vigorously shake hands with Pontius, sealing the deal. He did not understand why she giggled as she giggled as she shook his hand.

The townspeople experienced after-effects of the melodic trance. Dazed and groggy, they stumbled a bit as they walked down the road back to town.

When Snowy looked back at Pontius, he was on his hands and knees, scooping up the treasure with glee. She felt pity for him when kissed a gold piece. *What a wretched, greedy man!*

The townspeople were silent for some time, but as they reached the town square the mayor suddenly yelled,

"Hooray for you, little girl! You saved our lives!" He threw his arms around Snowy's shoulders.

Then the entire crowd came alive with happy shouts and cheers, and the mayor beamed, "What is your name, my dear?"

"I'm Snowy. I'm from Epping Forest." She smiled.

The townspeople gathered around Snowy in a frenzy of excitement. They went and retrieved instruments out of their homes, starting a celebration on the spot. Now dark out, a bonfire roared as they played the festive music. Others danced and chatted, but as the townspeople became more energized, Snowy became so sleepy she could barely keep her eyes open.

Just as Snowy was about to nod off to sleep, she saw a familiar friend ride up on the back of Shadow, the pony. "Minty!" she exclaimed.

The crowd parted to let Minty and Shadow pass through. Somehow, in just a couple of hours, Minty looked much better—well-rested. Her green eyes had regained their usual sparkle.

When Minty dismounted next to Snowy, she said, "You look very sick." Minty gently wrapped a cloak around her best friend. She opened a saddlebag on the pony and took out a jar of tea and a teacup. She poured the steaming hot tea into the cup. "Drink this tea that I've made for you. It will make you feel better."

Snowy drank, relishing the sweeter than normal chamomile tea. There certainly *was* something different about it. She licked her lips and sipped again.

"Snowy, when I went back to the ship, I was feeling horribly sick from whatever it was that Sneezie shared with us. One of the crewmen was brewing some tea and insisted that he share it with me, his new captain, before heading to bed. He was out of sugar though, and it tasted way too bitter.

"He tried so hard to make something that would comfort me, so I did my best not to hurt his feelings. I kept sipping the bitter tea, but then I remembered the chunk of glue bee honey that I had in my pocket. I decided the honey couldn't make the tea taste any worse than it already did, so I plopped it into my teacup. The tea tasted so much better! As soon as I finished, I realized I suddenly felt well again. It was amazing!"

Snowy believed what her friend was saying, because she was already feeling better, too. As she enjoyed the warmth from the fire the townspeople had built, she noticed the crew from the *Gillfish* had joined the celebration, and that made it even better.

"Ladies and gentlemen, hear me, please!" interrupted the mayor, who stood on a bench near the fire. In his loudest and most official voice he called out again. "Ladies and gentlemen of Southend-on-Sea, I have a very important proclamation!"

He cleared his throat, as an important person does before an important speech. "The town council, the bishop of Southend-on-Sea, and I, would first like to thank Snowy of Epping for saving us from the hands of Pontius Pilate. Because of this girl's bravery, sacrifice, and quick wit, we would like to announce that we will be knighting Snowy of Epping Forest. Forthwith, she will be known as a Knight Defender of Southend-on-Sea!"

The crowd applauded, crying out with glee. The mayor had to wait some time for the cheers die down before he could continue. "And a hearty thanks also to Snowy's friends from the *Gillfish*."

The mayor pointed to Minty and winked. Laughing, Minty made an exaggerated bow before the mayor.

The mayor smiled and said, "We would be honored if everyone would join us at this very spot at nine o'clock tomorrow morning, when the bishop will proceed with the official knighting of Snowy." He turned to where she sat on the bench, sipping tea. "The people of Southend-on-Sea are forever in your debt!"

The crowd cheered for Snowy, and the music played on.

CHAPTER TEN
OUTSMARTING OGRES

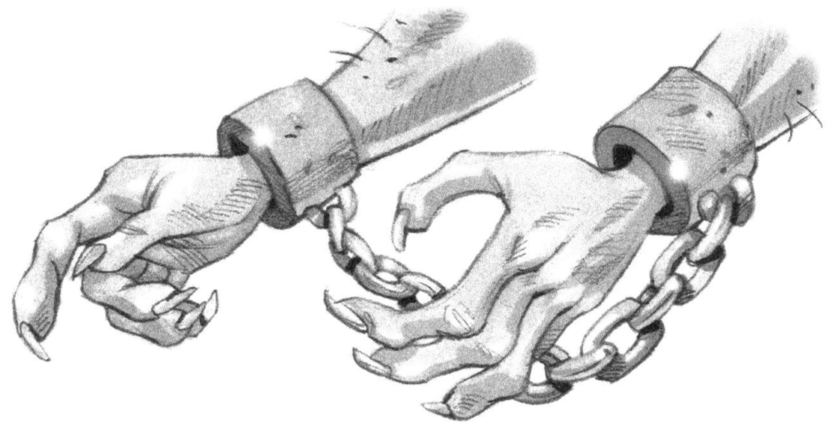

Snowy felt much, much better after drinking the tea that Minty had brought. The shine had returned to her bright blue eyes, as well as the pink in her cheeks. Thank goodness for the honey that so quickly helped her feel better!

At the appropriate time, Snowy stood up and thanked the mayor of Southend. Before they could get too deeply into conversation however, a distant commotion stole their attention. Everyone turned to see a long line of glowing lanterns moving quickly through the night, along the forest toward town.

"Hmm," Minty said, "those lanterns aren't walking by themselves!"

Both girls squinted, trying to see who was carrying the bobbing lights. Several of the shadows cast by the lamp light were familiar.

"They must be the townspeople of Epping," Snowy whispered excitedly to Minty. "They must still be escaping the ogres!" She jogged off toward the figures.

Minty, First Mate Carter, and a few others from the *Gillfish* crew hurried to meet them too.

The first face they saw was that of Mayor Carol. He was flushed from trying to keep ahead of the townspeople. Between panting breaths, he told the girls what was going on. "Minty! Snowy! The ogres are not far behind us, and they are angrier than ever! We stayed ahead of them only because you distracted them for so long."

With a last and mighty gasp, he plopped down right there on the road as others from Epping wearily walked past, going on into Southend.

"My townspeople could not move very fast, and our scouts reported just an hour ago that the ogres were catching up, hoping to devour us before we made it here."

Minty and Snowy looked in the direction from which the villagers were coming. Atop the dark outlines of the mountains, behind the villager's lanterns, they saw what looked to be large burning torches. The girls looked at one another, and with that single glance they each knew what the other was thinking. *The torches must belong to the ogres.*

"If the townspeople don't hurry, the ogres will probably catch up with the stragglers," Minty said. She looked at Snowy, and Snowy looked at Minty. They each gave a wink. They had an idea.

Snowy whistled for Shadow, which not only got the attention of the dark pony, but everyone else.

Minty addressed the crowd definitively. "First Mate Carter! I need you to organize a defense of Southend with every available man, other than Mr. Shepard and his team.

"Mr. Shepard, we have a special assignment for you and two others from the crew. We need you to load everything from Sneezie's bakery into a few wagons. Take the wagons to Pontius Pilate's warehouse as fast as you can manage. When you get there, convince Pontius to allow you to unload the wagon inside the warehouse. Tell him the stuff in the wagon is a final gift from Snowy and the grateful people of Southend.

"Mr. Clements," she winked, "take the remaining wagons and help the stragglers into town as fast as possible. We will distract the ogres, but we won't be able to do so for long. Ring the church bell when the last of the villagers are safely in town."

With that, Snowy and Minty climbed upon the back of Shadow and bolted up the trail. Mr. Shepard grabbed two of his mates, and they were off in a flash. First Mate Carter collaborated with the mayor of Southend to gather men and equipment as a defense.

As they passed along the weary line of Epping's townspeople, Minty and Snowy yelled out encouragement. "You're almost there, sir. Not far now! Warm fires ahead in town, miss. Keep on going, you'll make it!" When Minty saw a shivering little boy, she jumped off Shadow and wrapped him in her new captain's coat. He gratefully scampered about until his mother scooped him up and blew Minty a kiss of appreciation.

Minty and Snowy soon rode past Pontius Pilate's warehouse, and could see that lights were still on inside. They took that as a good sign. They were also happy that the line of Epping's townspeople was dwindling. Closer to the end of the line, several of the young men and women walked with the elderly too feeble to keep up with the others.

Back at Southend, even Mayor Carol, who had managed to get off the ground and walk again, carried a small girl on his shoulders. He huffed and puffed with exertion, but succeeded in keeping his short legs moving underneath his round body. The girl gleefully steered him by his ears and kicked him in the chest when his steps slowed.

When they passed the last person in line, Minty and Snowy were again on their own, and now in the chill of the night, heading toward some very angry ogres. The moon was just high enough in the sky for them to see the winding path. Both girls were thankful for that, because the light from their small lantern did little to illuminate the way ahead.

Farther up the hill was the dancing glimmer of torchlight, bouncing up and down with each big footstep. Booger was in the lead, torch in one hand and claw sword in the other. He was in an obviously foul mood.

The rest of the ogres were also mad. None of them had eaten for two days now. They blamed Booger *and* those annoying little girls.

"Look!" Booger pointed to the slow-moving lights of the townspeople ahead of them. "Getting close! Fresh meat before bedtime!"

Booger's promise was soon challenged, however. His torchlight revealed a little girl in the middle of the road, straight ahead. His heart sank. That little girl had been nothing but trouble for him, and the last thing he needed was more trouble!

Minty stood bravely, penknife in hand. When Booger's torchlight shone on her face, she looked the ogre in the eye and yelled "STOP!" with such force that they did exactly what she said.

The ogres stared at the little girl, stunned, and she stared back at them with determination in her eyes. No one said a word. The ogres remembered Minty's face from the church, when she was launching huge bags of powdered sugar at them. They remembered how she warned the townspeople to run away before becoming breakfast. They remembered how she dropped the bell on Krag and ignited powdered sugar into fireballs.

They also recalled how the girls had burned their food and stolen their treasure wagons, and how these same tiny, long-haired enemies had set up a trap to send a wagon full of boulders down the mountain to crush them.

Upon having such recollections, Booger shouted, "These are the worst little girls to ever live!"

Booger gazed down at Minty lips furled showing sharp, yellowed teeth. Minty was determined not to let Booger intimidate her. She glared at the ogre and snarled showing a combination of white baby teeth and larger permanent teeth, before adding a loud snort for emphasis. Everything was silent in the forest as the stare-down continued. As the tension mounted, Booger finally looked away.

The ogre named Mog pushed Booger aside. "If you no get her, I will!" he roared. He swung his torch like a club at

Minty. Minty was ready though, cartwheeling out of the way, off the trail, and into the bushes.

Then, the ogres heard another girl's voice from behind. "Ha-ha! You can't get me! You can't get me!" sang Snowy.

The ogres turned every which way, frightened at the sound of something moving in the bushes around them. Seeing only Snowy, one of the ogres in the back of the line lunged at her, but she, too, cartwheeled away into the bushes.

Suddenly, back in front, they heard Minty yell out, "Ha-ha! You can't get me. You can't get me. I belong to Pontius P.!"

The ogres noticed more movement in the bushes behind them and on each side of their group. They became confused, but Mog would have none of their games. Spying Minty through the bushes, he swung at her with fury. She jumped away, performing a round-off into the darkness on the left side of the path.

As the befuddled ogres began traveling up the road, they heard Snowy yelling up ahead on the right side of the road. "You can't get me. I belong to Pontius P."

"Stop saying that!" Booger yelled, as he swung his claw sword at her. Just then, jumping out of the darkness on the left, Minty darted to the back of Mog, and poked him in the backside with her penknife.

"Ouch!" Mog yelped, rubbing his offended rump.

Since his full attention was on Snowy, Minty ran behind Booger, who didn't know that Mog was crazily swinging his torch in her direction. Just in time, she dove expertly out of the way, and the torch landed squarely on Booger's back.

Pieces of torch wood and embers flew in every direction. Booger was stunned, and he spun around, accidentally clocking Mog with the side of the claw sword. Both ogres angrily reacted to their pain by punching each other in the gut.

"Ha-ha! You can't get me! I belong to Pontius P.!" taunted one of the girls.

The ogres were too dazed to know if it was Minty or Snowy who teased.

Mog and Booger growled some more at each other in fury, but quickly turned their attention back to the road. In the distance now also came the clanking sound of a wagon.

The ogres wondered how two girls could be in so many different spots all at once.

"You can't get me. I belong to Pontius P!" The girls' melody frustrated the ogres more with each repetition. Every time they came close enough to one girl, the other would jump out from behind a bush. Their travel toward Southend was becoming unforgivably slowed by the girls' antics.

Now the ogres were blinded by rage and thoughts of vengeance. They were determined to capture those pipsqueak girls.

Afar off, they heard the church bell ring loud and clear. At that moment, Mog and Booger realized what the girls were doing. They had done it again! They had been distracted, and were kept from getting what they wanted. The town had been warned, and the stragglers were now safely in town.

The bushes moved again, and this time Shadow bounded out of the darkness, galloping ahead to where Minty and Snowy stood on the road. Snowy grabbed a fistful of mane, vaulting herself up onto the pony's back. Minty took her friend's outstretched arm, and jumped up behind into a straddle.

Shadow galloped down the trail to Pontius Pilate's Pest Control. Arriving a short time later, the girls sent Shadow off, and stood alone in front of the warehouse door.

Trudging as quickly as their heavy legs would allow, the ogres eventually caught up with the girls, surrounding them in a half-circle. The ogres snickered and poked at them with their clubs. They were determined that the girls would not escape again. They would watch carefully for any tricks up their sleeves. Or so they thought...

Something deliciously distracting suddenly floated in the air. Their attention piqued, adrenaline pumping, they focused on the sweet aroma. Giant stomachs were growling like wild bears that had just awakened from a long hibernation.

Wondering where the scent was coming from, Booger looked up and read loud and slow the sign above the door, "Pontius Pilate's Pest Control."

As that was sinking in, the two girls pounded on the front door and said a little bit quieter now, "Ha-ha! You can't get me! You can't get me! We belong to Pontius P.!" They repeated the chant as the main door slid open, both Minty and Snowy pointing to Pontius as they chanted his name. Pontius stood there with a red nose, completely shocked.

The girls pushed the sliding doors open wider so all the ogres could see what was stored in the warehouse. As though in slow motion, the ogres' heads turned, and their eyes bulged at the sight of their two treasure wagons laden with gold. Their excitement increased as they saw the stacks of delicious cakes, cookies, and pastries from Sneezie's Bakery.

Pontius P. stood there petrified as Snowy grabbed the magic flute out of his shirt pocket. The girls dashed through the warehouse and out a small window in the back.

"They belong to Pontius P.? They belong to Pontius P.? Oh, do they?" Mog called out in a roar, "Get... HIM!"

Minty and Snowy scampered through the darkness of the woods for a while, then circled back onto the trail to Southend. When they whistled for him, Shadow reappeared, and they rode into town. As they approached the city's gates, they couldn't help but notice the excellent line of defensive barriers set up by First Mate Carter. He had constructed barricades of tables, benches, and an assortment of other objects in front of every opening in the town's walls.

Every able-bodied man, and even some women, stood ready to defend their homes and town. They were excited to see Minty and Snowy, and even more excited to hear their report.

From atop Shadow, Snowy yelled, "Ladies and Gentlemen, tomorrow morning before the ceremony, we will lead an expedition to Pontius Pilate's warehouse. There, we will find the ogres that attacked Epping, and will capture them without a fight. We will recapture the ransom we paid for Southend, and you will never see Pontius Pilate again!"

Upon concluding, she produced the magic flute that Pontius had used on them.

Seeing the flute so inspired the townspeople that they lifted the girls off of Shadow and paraded them from the defenses back to the city square on their shoulders. They danced and sang until the wee hours of the morning, but after just a bit of celebrating, the girls simply had to return to the ship for a ginger biscuit or two, a large pot of steaming hot chocolate, and a quick snuggle with Galileo before they settled in for a good, albeit short, night's sleep.

Before dawn the next morning, the town constable and a group of the strongest menfolk, traveled to Pontius Pilate's warehouse with Minty and Snowy. They opened the main doors to the wretched smell of sick ogres, finding just what Snowy had promised. Strewn around were heaps of half-eaten baked goods, alongside bloated purple bodies sniffling and sneezing.

The ogres were upset to find themselves surrounded, but far too ill to do anything about it. Their heads pounded with migraines, and their huge bellies rumbled with nausea. Booger, the leader, was passed out in a partially-eaten wedding cake, the small marzipan groom dangling out of his mouth.

There was no sign of Pontius Pilate. The wagons of gold and treasure were nearly untouched. The ogres had clearly been more hungry than greedy last night.

The constable put chains around the ogres, even though they seemed far too feeble to put up a fight, securing them thoroughly, using every lock they had in town.

CHAPTER ELEVEN
QUEEN LUVHONEY

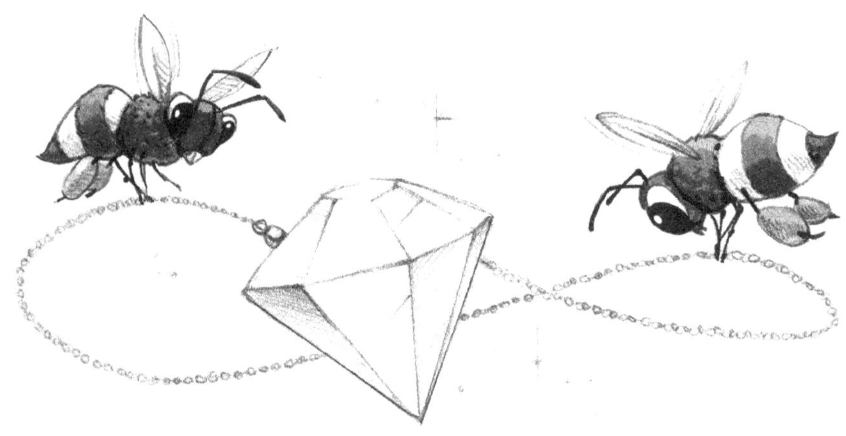

Minty, growing somewhat bored with watching the constable's work, strolled around the warehouse, and Snowy joined her. When they got to the back wall, they heard a faint buzzing sound. Where was it coming from? Below them? It was an eerie noise, deep and low. Both girls dropped to their knees, pressing their ears against the floorboards, trying to listen. They could feel the buzzing sound tickle their earlobes. The floor was vibrating!

"Do you think this is where the glue bees live?" Snowy whispered to Minty, whose face was only an inch from hers on the floor. "Pontius P. was somehow controlling them. He must have held them captive here."

They dusted off their knees and continued to search the warehouse, opening every door and drawer they could find.

When they looked inside a storage closet, they found the usual mops and brooms, but as soon as they opened the door, the buzzing became distinctly louder. Snowy closed and then opened the closet again, this time inspecting its back wall.

Minty scattered the brooms and mops onto the floor with a ruckus, and the buzzing momentarily stopped. Once it started again, it was even louder than before.

Snowy found a tiny latch on the back of the closet, and when she pulled it, the entire wall swung open. The dark closet was filled by a deep amber glow radiating from a secret room. The source of light hovered within an ornate birdcage—a large vibrant bee with glass-like wings.

Atop the bee's head sat a honey-colored crown, a red ruby at its center, and other jewels on each point. She wore a chain necklace from which dangled a shiny diamond. Smaller diamonds dazzled on bracelets around each of the bee's legs. In a dainty hand, she clasped a wand which shimmered in the amber light.

Minty grabbed Snowy's hand as they approached the bee. The girls could feel sadness emanating from the glue bee, and so they walked toward the cage slowly out of respect. Minty and Snowy came very close to the cage, beholding the full majesty of the queen bee.

The buzzing continued, softer now, almost like the purring of Galileo. The bee's giant eyes were the most sorrowful things the girls had ever seen. Snowy looked at Minty, and Minty looked at Snowy, and they both had the same feeling. Without a word, they unclasped the cage door, opening it wide.

"There you go. You should not be imprisoned," Minty whispered.

The bee extended her dainty legs to the edge of the door, then all at once jumped out with a flurry of her wings. She gracefully flew about the room in freedom.

After a few minutes, the lovely bee landed at the girls' side, and they leaned down as if expecting her to speak. The tiny agile legs of the queen took off the beautiful necklace that held the sparkling diamond, and extended it towards Snowy. Slowly, Snowy accepted it.

Upon taking the diamond, Snowy could hear in her mind what sounded like a thousand voices. She touched Minty, and Minty's eyes opened wide, as she could now hear the same thing.

"Hello..." One voice became clearest above the rest. "Thank you for freeing me. I've been Pontius Pilate's prisoner for over a year, and it feels so good to be loosed from that cage."

The bee fluttered her wings as if stretching them. "Hello?" she asked. "Children?"

"I can hear you," Snowy said out loud, hearing an echo in her mind. Without using her voice, she spoke again, this time with her mind, "I can hear you in my head, I think!"

"Yes, I can hear you, too. This is remarkable!" Minty chimed in.

"Yes, it is," the bee responded gently. "It is the power of the honey diamond that allows anyone who touches it to communicate with the world's bees.

"I am Queen Luvhoney from the Colony of Apis in Gall. I was captured by Pontius Pilate, and ever since, he's kept me under his control. Under the threat of harm, he has demanded that my children do his bidding all across France and England.

"Thank you so much for freeing me, children! In gratitude, I would like you to keep the honey diamond, so you can call upon me or any of the other bees in your land for help. We can be valuable allies in times of trouble."

Minty and Snowy thanked the queen for her kindness. Both were smiling excitedly, thrilled at all the amazing echoes that were floating through their heads.

"May I see my children?" Queen Luvhoney asked.

"Of course!" Minty and Snowy responded.

Snowy added, "We just need to figure out how to get to them."

Queen Luvhoney flitted about. "I believe if you look at the other wall in the closet, you will see a passageway to what is left of my colony."

The girls went back inside the closet, and on the wall they found another latch. It led to a passageway under the floor. They descended with excitement. Thousands of glue bees filled the basement, from one end to the other. Queen Luvhoney flew into the room, reuniting with her swarm blissfully.

Minty and Snowy were so overwhelmed by the many voices celebrating their queen's return that they had to leave.

As they entered the warehouse, they heard the constable say, "My ladies! We have been hearing such an awful buzzing of the bees that have plagued us, that we were worried about you!"

"It's all right, Constable," said Minty, slapping him on the back in a cordial manner. "The bees are our friends, and there is nothing to worry about."

"The bees were under Pontius Pilate's spell, too," Snowy added. "But now they're free, and they won't harm anyone."

"Aye, if only we had found that Pontius Pilot character here with these horrid-smelling ogres!" the constable said as he motioned to Mog to stay in line.

Minty and Snowy watched as the last of the sniffling ogres were shackled together, and then chained to the wagons. They were going to pull their own treasure back to Southend.

The girls said one last goodbye to Queen Luvhoney, still preoccupied with her many grateful children. They looked back, then looked at each other, and hurried to catch up to the guards who were leading the ogre prisoners.

Full daylight dawned. The sun shimmered across the landscape in happiness. As they got closer to town, Minty and Snowy heard a fanfare of trumpets, heralding the knighting ceremony. Minty was so very happy and proud for her dearest friend, wanting to get to the ceremony as soon as possible.

The townspeople reacted with awe as the guards, led by Minty and Snowy, walked cavalierly into town with ogres completely under their control.

"How did the girls manage *this*?" people asked one another.

"These girls are our heroes!" others said.

The constable locked the ogres in the jailhouse just in time to hurry back to the ceremony. Once the mayor spotted Snowy, he spirited her off to change into a special outfit, while Minty and the others stayed behind. As Snowy was led away, she turned and looked at Minty, and Minty looked at Snowy, and they each gave a wink.

CHAPTER TWELVE
CANNONS AND CRATES

Minty was famished and asked one of the council members if there was anything for her to snack on before the ceremony started. Embarrassed and red-faced, he explained that the town's food stores had been completely emptied by the raids of the glue bees, so there wasn't even a scrap of food anywhere in the town.

"As ordered by the bishop, we were going to wait until after the ceremony for everyone to go about getting more food. We can go without a further meal or two in honor of you and your friend."

Minty looked around, and could see expressions of hunger on otherwise joyful faces. The children's wide eyes made her realize she needed to get food for the townspeople right away.

Minty grabbed one of the sailors by the elbow and asked him to go to the *Gillfish*, check the storage rooms, and bring back all of the food he could find. "Distribute the food to the little children and the mothers of babies first," she said.

Within a short time, it was done. Minty looked on with great satisfaction, knowing that the hunger in her stomach was a good feeling in trade for the smiles of the well-fed and content children. She missed the warmth of her captain's coat, yet she was not cold. Her belly was empty, but she was not hungry any longer.

One of the town's councilmen escorted Minty to a place of honor, near the city well. This was where the knighting ceremony would take place. Drums and trumpets, and all sorts of fanfare soon came down the road.

Noblemen and soldiers dressed in armor and dashing ceremonial uniforms escorted Snowy to a compass rose inlaid in the stone of the town square.

Snowy was dressed in a fine silk tunic and gold leggings. The mayor's wife, who had five boys, had been delighted at the chance to curl Snowy's hair and pin it up in a lovely style. Minty thought Snowy looked as beautiful as ever.

The bishop looked very regal with the tall white mitre atop his head. After he was handed a sword by the mayor, he said, in a powerful and deep voice, "I've knighted many men over the years for valiant service and bravery in action, but this is the first time I've ever knighted a female, and not just a female, but a young girl!"

He shrugged. "Still, this brave, young girl has demonstrated all the qualities that make a knight great. We dare not withhold respect from one so courageous on account of age or gender."

With that, Snowy knelt to the ground and folded her hands. The Bishop touched the tip of the sword on each shoulder. "Arise and be welcomed, Sir, er, um… Dame Snowy of Epping Forest. For you are a noble knight and defender of Southend-on-Sea!"

Every man, woman, and child of Southend-on-Sea clapped and cheered, but before anyone could disperse, a colorful parrot landed on the top hat of one of the noblemen, squawking for everyone's attention. The crowd went silent.

The bird let out a noisy, "Aahrt, I come with a message! Aahrt, I come with a message to the people of Southend-on-Sea!

"The message is simply this. *I, Captain Savage, will destroy your city if you do not turn over the treacherous*

maidens Minty and Snowy, along with their wagons of gold, by seven o'clock tonight! Aahrt!"

The crowd was shocked to see that just inside the port loomed the large black ship, the *Fog*, belonging to Captain Savage. Cannons were ready on every deck.

"You have until seven o'clock tonight to turn them over! Aahrt!" With that, the bird leaped into the air and flew toward the dark ship, shouting, "Seven o'clock! Seven o'clock! *And in just seconds, you will see that I am very serious."*

The parrot circled higher and higher. Suddenly, the unmistakable sound of thundering cannons descended over the crowd. *Boom! Boom!*

Everyone scattered as cannonballs crashed into the town, hitting vacant stores and homes. There was immediate chaos and screaming.

Minty and Snowy leaped away from a nearby store, its walls and roof bursting into sharp shards of wood. They ran down the road that led to the pier. "We've got to get to the ship," Minty yelled.

"Yes, we've got to fire back!" Snowy yelled back. "Let's draw him away from the city so no one gets hurt!"

They dodged left and right to avoid more flying debris. Smoke belched from the cannons, and the church steeple took a direct hit.

The black ship was making its way out of the harbor now. Cannons started blasting the crew of one of the tea trading ships, the *Hawker.*

The navy ship, the *Troy,* gave chase, their crew scurrying to load their cannons.

First Mate Carter was already on the *Gillfish.* He must have seen the black ship before everyone else.

The girls ran headlong down the wharf's planks. Minty called out, "The *Gillfish* won't be ready in time! Most of the crew is still at the ceremony! She then pointed to the *Hawker.* "Looks like they could use our help!"

The *Hawker* had taken several cannonballs to one side. The decks were also severely damaged. Thinking fast, Minty snatched a line from a loading crane and grabbed Snowy's hand. In one smooth motion, the two swung out over the water, dropping squarely on its top deck. The crew was in a frenzy of disorder. The ship was taking on water at a rapid pace.

In the meantime, the *Troy* fired back at the pirate ship, but with so little time to prepare, they narrowly missed their mark.

Minty didn't see the *Hawker's* captain, so she ordered the crew to take instant action. "Men, we need to get this ship beached! I don't think she'll float long enough for us to save her. Get that main sail up! Now!"

The crew jumped to action at such an authoritative command. The main sail went up with slow creaks, soon followed by a *whoomph!* As it filled with air.

Snowy looked at the cargo hold below. Seawater was creeping in fast. The ship ponderously began to move toward the shore. Snowy clasped her hands together and prayed, "Lord, please bless this ship to stay together until it reaches safety."

Another battery of cannons fired from the dark ship, hitting the *Troy* squarely, creating more damage. Smoke billowed from the mangled ship as the fire on board grew.

Then the aft of the *Hawker* was struck with the tremendous crash of a cannonball. The ship lurched forward. "Oh no! They've hit the rudder!" called out the helmsman.

The *Hawker* moved closer to the shore. Jagged rocks threatened to take it down completely, framing either side of the sandy beach. With the rudder damaged, the ship suddenly took a sharp turn, approaching the shore sideways. There was a faint whistle from another cannonball, and in the next instant everything went black. Minty and Snowy were blown overboard into the cold sea.

Snowy reached for Minty and swam with her as they neared the shore. They pulled themselves onto the beach, and then watched with wide eyes as the *Hawker* crashed against the rocks, throwing its cargo and debris everywhere. They were once again barefoot. Their shoes had either slipped off during the explosion, or when they were swimming away in the aftermath of the crash.

Meanwhile, as the black ship slipped out of range, First Mate Carter took a small crew to help put out the *Troy's* fire. Once aboard, he was startled to discover that the ship was chock full of gunpowder! She must have been assigned to deliver the explosive cargo to the naval batteries up the coast. He tried to raise the main sail, to get them closer to shore, but several of the ropes were already on fire.

Fire bells suddenly clanged from town. Minty was exhausted, trying to catch her breath after the unexpected swim. She pushed her sopping wet hair out of her eyes, and as she did so, she noticed something strange. "Uh... Snowy," she said, "look there! That tea container is moving."

It was a large cargo box, appearing to walk all on its own, up the beach toward Main Street.

"That's not the only one!" Snowy said in astonishment. Several other pieces of cargo were marching in an orderly fashion just below the pier, and disappearing into a cave. They were heavy boxes full of tea, silk, and spices belonging to the now demolished *Hawker*.

The tired girls stood up and ran toward one of the large crates as it neared the cave.

"Hey, what's going on here?" Snowy demanded of the crate marked *Papa's Pepper—The Finest in Spices*. The crate halted and spun around. When the girls looked closer, they saw a tiny red leg sticking out from underneath.

"It's not yours," a small voice squeaked.

Minty stooped even lower and was amazed to see a dozen or more crabs.

A small but sharp voice called out in agreement, "Nope, this is property of the Crab King, recovered from the deep."

Minty answered back, "No, it's not! It's cargo from the *Hawker* that was just shipwrecked, and it isn't very polite to take advantage of a shipwreck!"

"No, it belongs to the Crab King!" the sassy little voice from beneath replied. "Leave it alone or you'll be arrested."

The crate continued moving forward to the cave's entrance. Minty and Snowy saw a long line of marching cargo already inside the cave. The girls didn't know whether to be amused or frightened.

"Not a chance, little crab!" Minty spouted. "That's not yours *or* his! It belongs to someone else."

Minty and Snowy grabbed at the crate, and could hear the strain of the crabs fighting to hold on.

"All right, human, have it your way!" A crab poked out, and pinched the toe of the barefooted Minty.

"Ouch!" Minty yelled.

Another crab pinched at Snowy's heels. "Yipes!"

The next thing they knew, a dozen crabs with prattling claws surrounded them. With nowhere else to go, Minty jumped on top of the crate and held a hand out for Snowy. Snowy accepted it, hopping onto the crate. The two sat lifting their knees to their chins, so the crabs could not nip their feet.

"Ha! As I said, this is the property of the Crab King. Now, you're coming with us."

As though choreographed, all the crabs converged on the crate. With a mighty heave, they lifted it up, girls and all, and the crate moved into the cave.

It was very dark inside, but their eyes soon adjusted. More cargo moved ahead of them and behind them. The air was damp and musty, and they heard the sound of running water. After a short time of bobbing along in the darkness, they came upon lit torches lining the walls.

The torchlight gave notice to silhouettes of thousands of crabs covering the ground. Minty and Snowy did not dare step off the crate now. As the *Papa's Pepper* crate continued on its strange journey, the cave opened into a large cavern, also lit by torches.

The crate came to a stop in the middle of the room, where the crabs dropped them off. In front of Minty and Snowy sat a large throne made of seashells and coral. On the throne sat a red-orange crab who clicked a gigantic claw. (This was no tiny crab. It was a monster of a crab—at least eight feet tall!) Beneath his gold crown, large, beady eyes focused on the girls.

There would be no escaping. Encircling the cavern stood six-foot-tall crabs with spears, fierce claws and grumpy dispositions.

Scattered around were cargo crates, barrels, netting, and boxes of every possible kind, some old and some new.

Crabs moved more crates to each side of the king as he spoke.

"Why are these humans here before me?" The king boomed, with a deep and frightening voice.

A small, bright red crab called out to him, "For attempting to steal the cargo that we rightfully rescued from the ocean."

"What? That's preposterous!" the Crab King responded with abruptness. "No one steals from me!" He snapped his monster claws in annoyance.

Snowy noticed something bobbing in some sort of pool behind the Crab King's throne. It was a bucket. Water sloshed out a bit as it quickly went up to some unseen destination, and then came back down just as fast. This happened over and over. Snowy whispered for Minty to look, but Minty had already spotted it.

"I will sentence you two to be eaten by me as soon as possible, and that will teach you!"

Snowy whispered to her friend, "We must be under the town square, and I'll bet that bucket is at the well."

"Yes," Minty agreed. "The townspeople must be getting water to put out the fire."

The Crab King could tell his captive audience was distracted. Why were they not taking his threats seriously? He expected the two little girls to be frightened, and at the very least, be crying by now. "Pay attention! I've decided to punish you by eating you...you human imbeciles! Do you

understand that?"

The girls half-heartedly listened. Just then, the smell of smoke entered the room, grabbing everyone's attention. One of the crabs scurried past the girls to investigate as a wave of small crabs flooded into the chamber. A loud explosion somewhere nearby boomed, causing the entire cave to tremble.

Minty looked at Snowy, and Snowy looked at Minty, and they each gave a wink. They knew this could be their only chance to escape!

CHAPTER THIRTEEN
THE INAUGURAL

As thick smoke billowed into the room, Snowy bolted behind the Crab King's throne, with Minty a half-step behind. Just as the bucket came down again, they dove into the pool of water, dodging the king's huge claw, and an attendant's spear.

Minty was the first to reach the bucket's rope. She extended a hand toward Snowy. Another spear flew through the air, splashing into the water beside them.

At the cavern's entrance, a fiery light grew, climbing the dried seaweed on its dirt walls. A stampede of more crabs burst inside in a frantic frenzy, crawling all over each other.

Snowy grabbed Minty's hand and the two steadied their positioning on the bucket. It lurched upward under the sudden weight. The crabs didn't notice them ascending, distracted by a sudden wall of fire entering the room.

Snowy looked up and could see some of the townspeople's faces peering down at them in surprise. She yelled, "Pull us up, faster!"

There was so much yelling, both from above and below. The girls watched thousands upon thousands of crabs climbing all over each other, over the guards, even over the Crab King.

Then came another explosion, sending more smoke inside the cavern. Its boom caused the bucket to swing about chaotically. They held on tight as heat built up around them. They gagged and coughed, unable to see each other.

Up, up, they went some more. The higher they went, the more they could see. Their eyes burned from the smoke, as they watched the stonework of the well pass before them.

Hands pulled them out just before flames shot up, igniting the bucket. Minty and Snowy could barely grasp that they were safely on the ground in the town square. While they hugged in relief, a plume of steam and smoke puffed from the well like a chimney.

It was an even more amazing sight around town! Several house fires, set by the black ship's cannonballs, were being put out by an unlikely combination of efforts. A brigade of men were tossing buckets of well water through windows, while thousands of glue bees poured gigantic honey-combs filled with sea water over the roofs.

When the townspeople realized what the bees were doing, their fear turned to respect and admiration. Without their help, they would surely have lost their homes, especially now that the well was suddenly out of service.

***

Once the smoke settled, the girls found out what happened while they ascended the well...

First Mate Carter had tried beaching The *Troy*, but the fire aboard grew completely out of control. Embers falling from the burning mast landed on the cargo hold, where the barrels of gunpowder were stored. That's when he ran as fast as he could. The blast was huge, catapulting him into the ocean.

He survived, pushed along just before the swelling tide that crashed the vessel under the pier, lodging its bow inside the cave. The power of the explosion rocked the town. Water rushed into the Crab King's cavern, and was quickly turned to steam by the massive heat generated by the explosion.

The Troy, and much of the pier it was lodged under, were completely destroyed. On a good note, some of the items from the Hawker were recovered, and everyone was overjoyed to find that no one had been killed in the attack.

Minty and Snowy were happy to learn First Mate Carter was okay. They helped put out the rest of the fires, then regrouped with everyone at the town square. Wounds were bandaged, while the last of the smoldering embers were snuffed out cold, thanks to the glue bees, bravely facing their fear of fire for the sake of the townspeople.

Minty looked at Snowy, and Snowy looked at Minty, and they each gave a wink. Then Minty whispered something in Snowy's ear.

Snowy stood up to get the attention of the mayor. "Mr. Mayor! Where is the nearest dairy farm in the area?"

Confused by the question, he took a moment to respond. "It's Mr. Saxon's farm... just a mile or so up the road. Why do you ask?"

"I would like for your four fastest horsemen to ride like lightning to the farm and bring as much fresh cream as they can carry back with them. Also make sure they grab every churn they can find along the way."

Everyone eyed Minty with puzzled expressions, so Snowy climbed to the top of the table to address the crowd.

"Ladies and gentlemen, we need these men to bring back the cream so we can churn it into butter." Her voice grew louder. "We need butter—for today, the entire town will feast! I am proud to announce that today is The Inaugural Southend-on-Sea Crab Fest!"

Snowy described the large crabs that lived beneath the city. Within minutes, men were lowered down into the well, and buckets filled with hundreds of large, steamed crabs were pulled back up. Curious adults and children gathered around them to see the succulently steamed creatures with deep red shells. Food, at last!

Tables and benches were brought out of nearby shops to sit and dine, and fresh cream was soon delivered by the horsemen, just in time for the mayor's first "Butter Churn-Off." Spectators laughed as burly men were beaten by their wives, who were more than familiar with the finer techniques of butter-making. The girls were delighted to see the winner was the young mother of the little boy to which Minty had given her coat on the long walk from Epping to Southend.

The town bustled with fun activity. Happy, hungry people rejoiced over the impromptu feast. The Crab King, being a special delicacy, was reserved for Minty and Snowy, who gladly shared with the town council. Minty prepared him with a super-secret spice rub and seasoned breadcrumbs, beside a thick, cheesy dipping sauce.

Sneezie even brought out cartloads of fresh-baked bread. Of course, nobody dared touch them until Mr. Shepard announced Sneezie had been completely cured, and by glue bee chamomile tea nonetheless. Even still, to take a confident bite, they needed assurance he was all better *before* baking... and that his work space was thoroughly sanitized.

Mr. Shepard was happy to declare his overseeing of every minute of the baking process. There were no "unwanted ingredients" in the bread.

The townspeople had one of the best and most festive days together that any of them could recall. However, one thing did weigh a bit on their minds...

"What will we do to meet Captain Savage's demands by seven o'clock tonight?" someone asked.

Minty looked at Snowy, and Snowy looked at Minty, and they each gave a wink. "No worries!" Minty exclaimed. "We have a plan. For now, let's celebrate!"

CHAPTER FOURTEEN
SAYING GOODBYE TO THE GILLFISH

As the feast wrapped up, everyone now stuffed with crab and crusty buttered bread questioned what to do about Captain Savage's demands. Do they turn over their new town heroes to the most evil pirate in the land, or would they somehow put up a fight?

The *Troy* had been their best defensive ship, and it was now a complete loss due to the explosion. Stories circulated that even its cannons were destroyed in the tremendous heat. Unfortunately, very little from the *Hawker* was salvageable.

At the directive of Snowy, the town explored the crabs' caverns, discovering many supplies, and even some treasures which had gone missing over the years, presumed to have been stolen by pirates. The rediscovered treasure was offered to Minty and Snowy for all of their help, but the girls generously refused.

Finally, when they knew they must answer all of the circulating questions, Minty looked at Snowy, and Snowy looked at Minty, and they each gave a wink.

Snowy stood up and addressed the crowd. "People of Southend-on-Sea, we thank you for your hospitality, and for the wonderful celebration and kind offers, but I need to ask just a bit more of you. Will you help us prepare to take on Captain Savage and his band of pirates? We know all the planning and teamwork in the world can only help so much in defeating the evil he has planned, but through our efforts and God's providence, we're sure to come away victorious.

Snowy continued, "This is what I ask of you. First and foremost, to live in peace with the glue bees, as they truly will do you no harm. They only want to live in peace. They were under Pontius Pilate's spell, but now they will be excellent neighbors. Secondly, we need the help of everyone in preparing the *Gillfish,* as we only have a short time to get her ready."

The mayor piped in, "You will have whatever you ask. Just tell us what you need."

Snowy smiled and jumped up to the top of the table so everyone could hear her. "Excellent! Thank you! Then let's get to work!"

"Lead on!" the mayor shouted to Snowy. "We are ready to do as you ask."

"First, we need to repair the section of the wharf that was damaged with the *Troy's* destruction, so we can easily move along the pier. Next, we need everything but the cannons and the cook stove removed from the *Gillfish*." Snowy continued with more orders, detailing how they should be carried out.

The entire town, including the refugees from Epping, jumped into motion. The *Gillfish* was completely unloaded and made ready. As for the ramshackle pier, doors were voluntarily taken off of local houses and used to patch the wharf. It would do until some proper lumber could be found.

Out over the sea, the townspeople suddenly saw a bank of familiar, mysterious fog gathering.

Minty commented, "It's probably Captain Savage spying on us... unless he decided to collect early on his demands."

Snowy and Minty called in the glue bees for some help. Within minutes, they swarmed on the starboard side of the *Gillfish*, coating it with a thick layer of honey. Two empty wagons had been loaded on the deck, draped with just enough jewelry to look filled with treasure. Honey was also deposited there, while the real treasure wagons were guarded at the mayor's house by the constable.

On the port side of the ship, two dinghies were laden with ropes and pulleys, so they could easily be lowered to the water below. The four main cannons were then loaded with two times the normal amount of gunpowder to each cannonball. Snowy knew just what they should do. With a little ingenuity, some tough chains, and a lot of strength, the crew pointed the cannons downward at the deck's wood flooring.

On the starboard side of the ship, the four main cannons were loaded, not with cannonballs, but with what resembled gigantic harpoons. They were heavy-duty poles with sharp points, tethered to long chains. The chains were attached in several places to the bulkheads, supports, and hull, giving them added strength. Snowy, being an inventor, appropriately named them spike cannons, for they were fierce!

The chained ogres, still terribly sick and extra grumpy, were prodded to the main cargo deck. There was no end to their grumbling, but they had no real energy to resist. At Minty's order, their weapons were gathered up and taken aboard. She had an especially fun time taunting Mog, by

prodding his rear with the tip of the claw sword. "Faster, you big oafs!" she called out.

Next, in the galley, Minty supervised the cooking of a large cauldron of chamomile tea, making sure to add her special ingredient—glue bee honey. "That'll do the trick," she said, sniffing its sweet, sweet fragrance.

Finally, the thick doors of the cannon ports were replaced with paper-thin wood. The *Gillfish* was ready, just as the sun settled lower in the sky.

The *Fog* was suddenly visible. It cut through the water with a supernatural speed, getting closer and closer to the pier. Everyone aboard the *Gillfish* stood, waiting to see what would happen. The dark fog out at sea grew heavy again, and Captain Minty announced it was time for the *Gillfish* to set sail, to face Captain Savage and his crew! The main sail rippled proudly, while the forward sail was tied firmly with a red rope attached to the release. A slight breeze favored the ship, taking her out to sea.

After sailing a short distance, Captain Minty announced, "My smart and brave men, it's now time for you to go back to shore!"

"Now?" First Mate Carter asked with a confused look.

"Yes!" Minty said as she put her hands on her hips and looked at him confidently.

"But we can't leave you here, Cap'n," another said.

"You must!" she said as she stood even straighter. "Now, take the dinghy there, and have faith. We have a plan."

Snowy crossed her arms across her chest, nodding with a smile.

The crew had to admit they had seen enough to know that Minty and Snowy would devise a brilliant plan. That plan just didn't include them. Finally, with some shouts of confidence, they followed orders and headed back to Southend.

Once Minty and Snowy were left to some quiet time alone, they suddenly felt so small out on the big, dark sea. A hint of fear and doubt swept over them as they thought about all that had happened. Even though they had brave hearts, they were still young girls...

They sat together, each on a barrel, silent for a moment longer. Then Minty looked at Snowy, and Snowy looked at Minty, and they both dropped to their knees.

They folded their hands on their laps, and Minty prayed, "Lord, you've protected us so much—from the ogres, the pirates, Pontius, and the crabs. You have protected the townspeople of Epping and Southend-on-Sea. Lord, you are so good to us! You've provided food when we were hungry. You gave the town of Southend-on-Sea crabs to feast on, just like you gave the multitudes in the Bible fish and bread to feast on when they were hungry…"

Snowy added, "You healed us with the chamomile tea when we were sick. We are so grateful."

"Yes," Minty prayed in agreement. She said, "Lord, now we face a brutal enemy that we know would like to destroy us. We ask that You protect us once again, and work out all things so that You may be glorified.

"Our enemies are a band of destructive pirates, and we are but two young girls. They are strong, but we are weak. They are many, but we are only two. Lord, we know that all things are possible with You. We ask that You stand with us today so that all might know that You are God."

The girls prayed for several more minutes, and when they stood back up, there was a break in the overcast sky. The bright amber light of the sun shone down upon the deck of the *Gillfish*. Both girls were bathed in its warm glow.

They looked at each other and smiled. The shadows of doubt and fear that had spread across them was now gone. They looked with confidence to the horizon, not in fear of the black ship's approach. They knew something amazing was about to happen.

***

The pirate ship emerged from the fog. Captain Savage had a good view of the *Gillfish*, as it was clearly visible in the evening light. His scarred face gave a slight smile at the lone ship in the distance. Obviously, the townspeople had made the right decision to turn over the girls... and the treasure.

Captain B. T. Rayer was now second-in-command on the dark ship, and he looked with determination upon his old ship, the *Gillfish*, hoping to take her back and get revenge on Minty and Snowy for humiliating him.

The *Gillfish* was out of range of being rescued by any other ship or any battery of cannons from the shore. The ship, treasure, and girls were alone and ripe for the taking.

***

Minty and Snowy knew they were being spied on. They dashed about the ship making their final preparations for the ensuing battle.

The firing hammers on each of the eight cannons were pulled back and a wedge of wood was placed in each one.

The wedges on the four spike cannons were each tied to a blue rope. The rope was carefully trailed along the floor, and up the passageway to the starboard side's main deck.

The wedges on the cannons that faced downward were tied to another rope, a newer rope. This rope was threaded along the passageway and placed next to the doors to the cargo area.

The pirate ship moved closer to the *Gillfish*, and while the girls were a bit nervous, mostly they were confident. They went above deck. Knowing that the captain was spying on them, Minty and Snowy stood atop the pile of fake golden treasure, and put on their best sad faces, as if they were little girls who had been given up by the townspeople.

Minty even threw herself on Snowy, as though she had fainted under the stress of the situation. Snowy waved her handkerchief over Minty's face, while trying not to laugh at the theatrics.

Once the dark ship moved close enough though, the girls knew their situation was not the least bit funny. They feared the pirates might see the treasure was phony. Calling upon their bee friends by using the magic of the honey diamond, hundreds of glue bees took flight, buzzing toward the pirate ship.

The crew of the *Fog* was startled as the huge bees hovered about them. Their plan to distract the evil captain and his crew was working. The crew could no longer spy on the *Gillfish*.

When Captain Savage looked back, the girls had disappeared from view, but not the treasure wagons.

Unbeknownst to the captain, Minty and Snowy had gone below deck, and together they carried the heavy cauldron of chamomile tea from the galley to the cargo bay. The stench of the sickly ogres was nearly overwhelming. They placed the cauldron in the very center of the room, where the sweet smell instantly piqued their attention.

"Listen up, ogres," Minty said. "We don't really belong to Pontius P. We belong to the pirate, Captain Savage, and we're going to turn you over to him as our prisoners. Since we are kind girls, we wanted to give you a nice cup of tea to make you feel better before you are destroyed."

Minty took a ladle, filled a tin cup for each of the ogres, and placed them just within reach of their chained hands. The smell of the tea must have made them feel a little better. They growled and sneered at Minty and Snowy, the fire of anger returning to their eyes.

Minty and Snowy left at once. As soon as they were out of the monsters' sight, they heard the clang of tin cups. They imagined the ogres gulping down the tea breathlessly. Minty closed the door to the cargo area, and tied the new rope firmly to the handle.

The *Fog* came closer, turning so that it almost touched the *Gillfish* side-to-side. They were preparing to board the ship, claim the treasure wagons and capture the girls who had caused them so much trouble.

Minty waved her arms to get the pirates' attention, while Snowy went unseen to the starboard side of the ship. Snowy lowered the last dinghy into the water.

The *Fog's* crew was ready, swords pointed, to jump aboard the *Gillfish.* Meanwhile, there came a brash sound of clanking metal. Below deck, the ogres were ripping off their chains with newfound chamomile-honey-infused strength.

Just three feet shy of the *Fog* touching the *Gillfish,* came a roar from below the deck. When they were only two feet away, the pirates heard the pinging of chains being tossed to the floor. As the ships finally touched sides, instead of feeling a bump upon impact, the *Fog* stuck to the side of the *Gillfish.* The glue bee honey was doing the trick.

Minty ran to the red rope and tossed it over the starboard side, into the waiting dinghy. Captain Savage glared suspiciously at Minty, and Minty glared back, while Snowy handed her friend the blue rope.

"Ready, Snowy?" Minty asked.

"You bet," Snowy answered with a spark of excitement in her eye.

Minty and Snowy jumped off the side of the *Gillfish* just as Captain Savage yelled, "Get them!" to his boarding party.

As the rope played out, the four wedges from the spike cannons were removed. They fired at point-blank range into the side of the *Fog.* Both ships rocked, as the pirate ship was pierced deep into its belly.

The girls had landed hard into the dinghy, but sat right up to paddle away.

Captain Savage was greatly surprised by the first round of cannons, but that was only the beginning. The next round was much louder, the cannonballs bursting through a series of decks and out the bottom of the *Gillfish's* hull.

As the girls continued paddling, they heard more breaking wood and clattering metal aboard the *Gillfish.*

The huge shapes of furious ogres emerged from the cargo hold, snarling at Captain Savage. They were armed with their weapons and ready to fight. Everyone from the pirate ship gave a collective shout of terror and stopped, frozen in fear.

Minty and Snowy paddled safely away from the *Gillfish,* and came to the end of the red rope. With a forceful tug, Minty let the line go. The girls watched the main forward sail drop. On it was written in huge charcoal black writing, *Ha Ha! You can't catch me!*

Snowy and Minty laughed as several of the glue bees buzzed down, grabbing onto the side of the dinghy. They used their wings to help them speed back to Southend.

They watched as the *Gillfish*, now in the far distance, took on water. Because she was glued to the *Fog*, both ships were listing hard to one side. The damaged *Gillfish* had become an anchor, dragging the *Fog* down.

One of the crew shouted, "We're attached, and we can't break free!" Even as they were sinking, there was the unmistakable sound of clanking swords, as the pirates fought against the ogres in a desperate battle.

The mystic, dark fog that always hovered around the pirate ship grew thicker, and was almost green, obscuring things.

The last sound Minty and Snowy heard was in broken ogre English.

"Booger, you da worst leader ever!"

Snowy looked at Minty and said, "You were a wonderful captain for the *Gillfish*, my friend. I'm sorry that we had to leave the ship. Nevertheless, once a captain, always a captain! You're a great leader."

The girls waved goodbye to the *Gillfish* and continued on toward town.

Minty and Snowy returned to a hero's welcome in Southend-on-Sea. Snowy was presented by the town council with a suit of fine silver armor, made in just her size.

The best friends and the crew of the *Gillfish* were invited to stay the night at the mayor's house.

Within a few days, the girls were finally back home in Epping, where they enjoyed a long rest in their own beds. The two wagons of real treasure came with them, and both girls knew just what they would do. Snowy would have the *Gillfish II* built for Minty, and Minty would buy a new telescope—perhaps a very nice one from Germany—for Snowy. Then, they would simply go back to living ordinary lives until their next adventure was ready to unfold.

About the Author

Justin Mitson's debut children's book, *Starry Night Surprise,* is a love letter to his daughters. It is the written version of a story that he made up for them on the way home from a long camping trip when the radio wouldn't work. This story became part of a series of bedtime stories that lasted years.

Justin Mitson is an engineer and manager for a semiconductor company in Boise by day, and a dedicated entrepreneur and freelance writer by night. Born in Butte, Montana, he spent most of his childhood roaming around the Northwest, living in dozens of different locations before getting through high school. He married Lorna, his amazing chemical engineering wife, when he was nineteen. They graduated together from Montana State University in 1996. They live now in Boise, Idaho with their two daughters.

Learn more about Justin Mitson at www.redteamink.com, or add him as a friend on Facebook.